Halos and Horns

Sanjana M. Vijayshankar is a copywriter born in Bangalore, and based in Chennai. She dabbled in tax for a year before deciding to play with words for a living. When she's not scribbling away in a little red diary, she can be found behind volumes of Terry Pratchett's Discworld series, with her fingers wrapped around a cup of coffee.

Halos and Horns

SANJANA M. VIJAYSHANKAR

Published in Red Turtle by
Rupa Publications India Pvt. Ltd 2017
7/16, Ansari Road, Daryaganj
New Delhi 110002

Sales Centres:
Allahabad Bengaluru Chennai
Hyderabad Jaipur Kathmandu
Kolkata Mumbai

ISBN: 978-81-291-4453-9

First impression 2017

10 9 8 7 6 5 4 3 2 1

For my Mathematics teacher, Lochani Subramanian,
who taught me a lot more than just numbers

Contents

Prologue

I never believed in ghosts. It was Rishi's idea to perform the 'Summon a Demon' ritual on a pitch-dark night. Near a railway track. Genius.

'We have to cross the tracks to get to that lawn,' said Pranav, who was riding his motorbike beside mine.

'You don't say,' I muttered. I couldn't have made it clearer that I wanted to play no part in mobilizing some non-existent demons to Earth. But my voice was lost in the dwindling rumble of Pranav's motorbike.

'Isn't there a railway crossing?' asked Shirley, bringing her Vespa to a halt next to mine.

Rishi shook his head as he got off Shirley's Vespa. He extracted a piece of paper from his jacket.

'Is that the incantation?' I asked, even as thoughts like 'this is so lame' flashed through my mind.

'Yeah,' said Rishi. 'I got it off the Internet.'

'Which website?'

'I'd rather not say.'

'Because it's stupid?'

'No,' snapped Rishi, folding the piece of paper and pocketing it. 'Because I sense you don't completely believe in this.'

'Ah, you *sense* it now, do you?' I smirked as we trudged along.

Rishi's face was hidden in shadow, but I could tell he was scowling.

'This is stupid, Rishi,' I said, following him to the said lawn skirting the tracks.

'Shut up,' he hissed. 'Pranav, do you have the melting candle?'

'Yeah, man!' Pranav brandished an orange candle as if it were the Olympic torch.

'Um, don't *all* candles melt?' I asked.

Rishi opened his mouth to retort, but Shirley cut in.

'Aru,' she said, in her calm voice. 'Let him be. The idiot wants to do this; best to just go with it.'

'But we're twenty years old!' I protested as we all sat down on the hard ground which had been made wet by the evening's downpour.

'So?' snapped Rishi. 'Just hand me the bamboo shoots.'

'Were you hoping to feed some wild panda here?' I held out a small carton we'd brought along.

Rishi looked like he'd been struck on the head with a club.

'Eh?' he said thickly.

'The bamboo... Pandas like bam—never mind,' I said,

catching Shirley's eye. She was right. If Rishi had set his mind to something, he would do it. As stubborn as he was idiotic, he was unshakeable in his resolve to pursue all nonsensical things with a dedication his mother wished he'd show for his studies.

'OK,' said Rishi, arranging the sticks in a star-shaped pattern. 'Pranav, place the candle in the centre…there. Excellent!' he added as Pranav lowered the candle with theatrical deliberateness.

Shirley and I watched as the boys lit the candle, and sprinkled some water in and around the star from a crumpled water bottle. Rishi was muttering the incantation while he proceeded with the 'ritual'. I didn't trust myself with speech; all my energy was focused on suppressing may snort of laughter.

The flame hissed and flickered.

'See!' exclaimed Rishi. 'The flame protests! The light fades! The demon approaches!' He gazed at the moonless sky as if waiting for a portal to appear from where the winged fiends would descend.

I marvelled at Rishi's innate ability to turn something as moronic as a summoning game, designed for rowdy children or witless adults, into a dramatic event.

'Look at how the flame almost died, guys!' he looked around at us, his eyes bright and excited. 'This is surely an indication of the awakening of a demon!'

This was too much for me. The snort escaped my nostrils before I could stop it.

'Someone alert all Chemistry majors, please! The reaction between water and fire has now been renamed as "the awakening of a demon".'

Rishi shot me a look of pure venom. 'Get up and leave if you're not interested!'

Now, normally, I would've smacked Rishi playfully on the head and asked him to get along with whatever ludicrousness he had started, but it was the sheer bitterness in his voice at that moment which really got to me.

'Fine!' I said, and rose to my feet. 'This is absolute rubbish anyway! I can't believe you dragged me away from *Doctor Who* for this!'

Shirley tugged at my jeans. 'Aru, please,' she said. 'Don't go!' She turned to Rishi angrily. 'You idiot! Why do you have to be such a baby?'

Rishi said something, but I barely heard him as I was already storming off, away from my friends, and towards the railway tracks.

'Aru, come back!' shouted Pranav, his deep voice echoing across the empty station.

'Please, Aru!' Shirley called.

'I was kidding!' Rishi screamed, trying to coax me back.

But I didn't break my stride. I was angry, my eyes were burning and my nostrils were flaring. Rishi was a moron, and the other two were morons, too, for indulging him, I thought angrily.

Kicking up loose gravel as I marched across the lawn, I stepped onto the tracks and prepared to cross the lines and head home.

And that's when it happened.

My friends were yelling something, their tone more urgent now. But a faint buzzing was filling my ears. Had my anger dulled my senses? Then—

'Arundathi, watch out!' Shirley screeched.

I heard her warning at the same time I heard the chugging sound, and I saw the lights. In sheer terror I stood rooted to the spot, my eyes as wide as saucers and my legs leaden.

The last things I remember were the bright lights of the speeding train, the terrified voices of my friends beyond the tracks, and the sound of a dull thud as cold, hard metal crashed into my body.

I never believed in ghosts.

Not until I became one.

1

Misty Beginnings

The mist was everywhere. It was above me, beside me, all around me.

I'd opened my eyes about ten minutes ago, and thought that perhaps with each passing minute this unnaturally thick mist would dissolve, but it lingered. Needless to say, after spending about thirty seconds inside a dense fog, the novelty had worn off, and I was now beginning to feel annoyed.

I suddenly realized I was lying down. Groaning slightly, I sat up and glanced around.

Where am I? I wondered. Wait, who am I? What's... what's my name?

A horrible pang of panic filled me, shooting through my annoyance and confusion. I couldn't remember my name. Was I concussed? Where on earth had I hit my head?

I gulped hard and shook myself mentally. I'm dreaming,

I told myself. Let's just get out of here and finish watching that episode of *Doctor Who*.

My jaw set, I punched the mist, but in vain. I even tried doing something with my arms which might have resembled karate if I weren't actually twitching like a bug that had just seen the wrong side of a boot. I ran (or did something which felt like running), but it got me only from one mist-filled void to another. Like I said—it was *everywhere*.

'Stop flailing your limbs like that; you look like an epileptic octopus,' said a voice drawled behind me.

I spun around. And felt my jaw drop.

I stood facing a very strange man. Everything about him, right from his mop of curly hair down to the sandals he wore, was an equal mix of red and gold. He looked like a mascot for a sports team, painted to reflect its jersey colours. He was short and skinny, and seemed to be buzzing with a kind of energy I'd never seen before in a living person. He held a clipboard in his hand, which he was tapping with a pen that sent wisps of green ink flying into the mist.

Also, he was floating. Literally *floating*!

'Yes, I can levitate,' said the strange man in a bored sort of way.

I must've looked like a concussed troll, gaping at him with my half-open mouth.

'W-who are you?' I stammered.

'I am the Middler, of course,' he said.

My expression cleared. 'Right, that explains everything, thanks.'

He smiled dryly. 'Don't give me cheek, girl.'

'Sorry,' I said, not feeling apologetic at all. 'So, you're a meddler?'

'Middler,' he corrected.

'Sure,' I shrugged. 'That's what I said.'

The man looked mildly irritated. 'Are you being difficult on purpose?'

'Yeah, I think I might be,' I said, distractedly. 'Where are we? What is this place?'

'You're in Nowhereland.'

'Eh?'

'Nowhereland! Aether, Ether, the Void…' the Middler said impatiently.

'The Void?' I raised an eyebrow, looking around at the brightness. 'I thought the Void would look like a dystopian fantasy, know what I'm saying? Black holes, burning plains and miscellaneous undead beings chomping each other and stuff.'

'Oh, how jolly that would be,' drawled the Middler. 'And before you hasten to paint a larger, more inaccurate picture of dystopia,' he hurriedly consulted his clipboard. 'Are you Rohini Kumar?'

'No,' I said, my eyes searching for a star that might be consuming itself.

'Sunaina Prasad?'

I shook my head. Still no imploding star... Weird. Just this bizarre mist everywhere...

The Middler hugged his clipboard. 'Then you must be Arundathi Jayaram.'

All thoughts of self-destructing stars and puffs of unnaturally thick mist were extinguished at the mention of that name. Arundathi. *Arundathi.* That rang a bell.

'Uh...' I began.

The Middler nodded vigorously. 'Yes, yes, you have to be her. You've rejected the first two names, and there have been only three untimely deaths in the last few hours.'

'What deaths?' I squeaked.

'Untimely.'

'I heard you the first time.'

'Then what's the confusion?'

'What do you *mean* untimely deaths?'

'Well, the traditional definition of death is the termination of life,' said the Middler, as if illustrating a recondite theory. 'Thus, untimely death would mean the premature termination of life.'

'I know what it means!' I snapped.

'You *just* asked me what it meant.'

'What *manner* of untimely deaths?' I asked loudly. 'Whose?'

'Rohini Kumar, accidental ingestion of rat poison (or her own cooking, ha ha). Sunaina Prasad, jumped off a building...'

the Middler rattled off.

'How can you be so cavalier about *death*?' I yelped.

The Middler seemed not to care as he continued to speak. 'And *you*, Arundathi Jayaram, hit by a train.'

His words rammed into my brain with the force of a thousand charging oxen.

'WHAT? That's not possible! I can't be dead!'

The Middler sighed in exasperation. His face bore a this-happens-every-day look.

'Think back, girl,' he said simply.

'I was hit by a train?' I wondered aloud. 'But I don't even...OH!'

It all came flooding back. My mind exploded with unpleasant, painful memories. A cold Sunday–midnight–Rishi, Pranav, Shirley and me–'Summon a Demon'–bamboo shoots–a scented candle–the railway tracks–a bunch of blinding lights–a thud.

I gulped, and forced my gaze downward. My feet were gone! I was floating! So were my shoes, my beloved Puma shoes for which I'd paid a fortune. My body ended in a wisp of vapour, which resembled feet. My jeans had turned white, so had my top. I could make out the floral patterns on it, but they were barely visible through a blackened patch on my torso. It looked horribly like a stain, a blood stain. Like I'd been struck by something. A train, maybe?

I held out my hands in front of my eyes. They were

translucent, pale white. I was as pale as a…

'Ghost,' nodded the Middler, as if he had read my thoughts.

I slowly looked up at him with eyes that were now quickly welling up, more out of panic than acceptance. What kind of sick joke was this, and who was playing it?

'So, I am…dead?' I absently wiped my cheeks.

The Middler cocked his head sideways and regarded me with a strange look in his eyes. Was it pity?

'Yes, I suppose you are quite dead.'

Something inside me jerked awake.

'*Quite dead*?' I shrieked. 'Then reverse it, dude! Do something and send me back! Use magic, voodoo…a…a reversal app, whatever! I cannot be dead! I *refuse* to be dead! I have things to do!'

'Er, what things?' asked the Middler, scratching his head with the end of the pen.

'STUFF!' I yelled, wishing I had something to throw at this bicoloured freak. 'I HAVE TO CROSS THINGS OFF MY BUCKET LIST! I HAVE TO *MAKE* A BUCKET LIST FIRST! I HAVE TO MEET A.R. RAHMAN AND CLICK A SELFIE WITH HIM! I HAVE TO HIT AT LEAST 50,000 FOLLOWERS ON TWITTER! I WANT TO WITNESS CASSETTES MAKING A COMEBACK! I WANT TO SLIDE DOWN A BOWLING ALLEY! I WANT TO GO ON A COLDPLAY TOUR!'

The Middler let out a low sigh.

'Pick another band, and we'll see if I can get you a return ticket to Earth.'

I didn't know whether to cry or thump this man. I sated myself with punching the mist again.

'AARGH!'

'Don't punch the clouds,' the Middler warned.

'We're inside a cloud?' I asked, breathing heavily and momentarily side-tracked.

'What did you think? That this was the world's largest white cotton candy?'

'There isn't any white cotton candy.'

'If you know where to go, you'll find them,' the man said sagaciously. Then he cleared his throat. 'Enough chit-chat. I have to take you to the Choosing Commons. So, follow me.'

'I'm not going anywhere with you,' I said loudly. 'This is all very bizarre, and I'm not even convinced I'm a dead girl, let alone a ghost. In fact,' I drew myself up, 'I'm pretty sure I'm dreaming, and any second now, my grandmother is going to wake me up with a cup of coffee.'

The Middler licked his lips. It looked as if he were trying very hard not to leap forward and slap me. I'd seen that sort of look from my Physics teacher many times.

The Middler spoke to me in steel-cold voice, 'Arundathi, I know this is hard to swallow, but listen carefully.' His eyes narrowed to slits. 'I have indulged your impertinence thus far. However, if you continue to use your slow realization of death as an excuse for subjecting me to your childish effrontery, especially when there are important people waiting for you behind these walls…' he motioned vaguely behind him, 'you will find out just how fast ghosts can burn.'

I swallowed hard. My mind raced. Ghosts can burn. Ghosts can burn? *Arundathi, ghosts can burn!* 'Lead the way,' I said.

The Middler's lips twitched.

'Wise choice.' He beckoned towards a meandering path which materialized the moment he raised his hand.

As we drifted along the bricked pathway, I looked around.

The path was fenced on one side with smooth, neatly laid pebbles, with freshly mowed lawn bordering them, dotted by daffodils and sweet-smelling jasmine flowers in full bloom. In the distance, I saw mountains, their golden peaks glinting. At their feet stood tall oaks, whispering in the wind. A sudden symphony sounded in my ears and sparked something in me, if only for a fleeting moment. A fire. It felt a lot like hope. I couldn't be sure, but it felt very much as if the music was coming from within me.

On the other side, there were rough, jagged rocks. They were jet black, and looked meaner than barbed wire fences. Thick, grey smoke rose in spirals between them, hissing menacingly. The ground quaked, spitting up small pools of magma which meandered through the gaps between the rocks, threatening to spill onto the path. Dark clouds grouped closer together overhead, and just the sight of them aroused a horrible feeling in me—I couldn't shake off the urge to cause pain, widespread and calamitous.

I found myself being drawn to both sides with an equal force. I wondered what that was all about.

Speeding, I caught up with the Middler ahead.

'What's this funny magnetic pull I can feel around here?'

He raised his eyebrows. 'Excuse me?'

'I can feel a strange pull from these fences and beyond,' I explained.

'Ah, that,' he grinned in a mysterious way. 'You'll find out soon enough.'

I clicked my tongue impatiently. 'Couldn't you just tell me now?'

'And where's the fun in that?'

'At least *one* of us is having a good time,' I grumbled.

We continued down the path, crossing a vast stretch of strawberry fields and a stinking quagmire.

'Where are we going?' I enquired.

'To a place that won't, ah, *cloud* your senses,' said the Middler, chuckling appreciatively at his own joke.

I made an impatient noise. 'Just tell me.'

'I did, you dolt—the Choosing Commons. You get to make a judgement call.'

'Er, on what?'

'Your fate.'

'You mean I can go back to being alive if I'm actually dead?' I asked with a hint of longing.

'Rid your thinking of such impractical expectations,' said the Middler loftily. 'Nothing can send you back to your mortal shell.'

I couldn't mask my disappointment. 'So, you're saying I'm irreversibly dead, then?'

'You seem a bit soft in the head,' the Middler said, squinting at me. 'Which syllable in "impractical expectations" escaped your grasp?'

I did my best to avoid looking at my see-through hands. The brief silence was filled with the sound of babbling brooks and gunfire.

'Hey, why couldn't I remember my name before you said it?' I frowned at the Middler.

'You took quite a hit from that train,' he explained. 'Such a collision often results in temporary abandonment of memories, thoughts, body parts...'

'What's that now?'

'Oh yes, we've seen loads of Disjoints here,' he nodded. He caught the bemused look on my face. 'I mean ghosts who've detached themselves from their human form without a nose, toe, spleen...you get the picture.'

I felt nauseated.

'What's your role as the Middler?' I piped up after some time.

The Middler took his time answering. He didn't look too pleased with my incessant chatter.

'I manage the passageway between the B's and G's.'

'The Bee Gees?' I said, a foolish giggle bubbling to my lips.

'No, because you're not exactly "Stayin' Alive", are you?' he grinned nastily.

I resisted the urge to strangle him.

On my left, a spectacular garden of red tulips swayed in the wind. But from my right came the stench of a polluted lake that made me screw up my nose up into a knot. I felt dizzy. So dizzy, in fact, that I was imagining a flying chariot coming our way.

The chariot was a brilliant shade of orange, like it was made of sunset. It didn't seem to need any form of assistance from horses or any other quadruped because it was pulling itself slowly through the air. Has everything and everyone in this place adopted a firm anti-gravity policy, I wondered.

I shot a sideways glance at the Middler. His lips had formed a straight line and a frown creased his forehead. It couldn't have been clearer that he could see the flying chariot too, and that he was most displeased.

The Middler and I halted as the chariot inched towards us. The man riding it seemed to be immersed in a sheaf of papers, wearing deep frown lines that seemed unlikely to abandon the company of his forehead for a long time.

I wanted to get off the path so as to avoid the chariot

wheels, but flattening the tulips seemed as bad an option as did stepping into the putrid lake. I hurriedly took refuge behind the Middler. The hovering chariot was on the verge of making contact with his forehead when he finally decided to clear his throat loudly and pointedly.

The man riding the chariot brought it to a halt and looked up from his papers. Spotting the Middler seemed to act like a Botox shot, because the lines that had creased the man's forehead just moments before disappeared magically.

'Hi there!' he said cheerfully, and jumped out of the chariot with more grace than I'd expected.

'Hello,' replied the Middler, rather stiffly.

The man wouldn't have looked completely out of place at a rock concert, I noticed, with his leather jacket and high boots. His stringy hair ended in the tiniest ponytail. The only thing about him which complemented his choice of transport was the bow and arrow slung across his shoulders.

'Off on business, I presume,' said the Middler to the man, coldly. For some reason, his tone made the surroundings so cold, a sleuth of polar bears could've marched right through.

'Right-o!' The man beamed, pocketing the sheets of paper which had had him so engrossed only a moment ago.

The Middler grimaced. 'What happened to the Rolls Royce?' he asked.

'Ah.' The man scratched his neck, looking slightly abashed. 'Dented on duty.'

'Dented on duty,' repeated the Middler.

'Yes, slightly,' nodded the man.

'This dent...' the Middler asked, 'is it noticeable?'

'Only if you press your nose up to the car really close,' the man replied, laughing nervously.

'Well, what's another crater on the moon, right?' said the Middler, his tone colder than ever.

I didn't understand why the man wasn't wetting his pants. The Middler was giving him a look as though he wanted to give him an excruciating facial rearrangement. But no, the man continued to grin and prattle away.

'I was swerving around a bend in the road, and a buffalo darted out in front of the Rolls–' he explained, but the Middler cut him off.

'Buffaloes don't normally *dart* about, you know.'

The man blinked. 'Well, in any case,' he said hastily, 'I wanted to avoid hitting it, because the last thing I need is for an engineer to quit his job and become a "professional animal rights blogger" like that's an actual career, you know? So, I...er...crashed the car into a...er...lamp holder thing.'

'A lamp-post,' the Middler said.

The man snapped his fingers, 'Exactly!'

'I'll pay damages,' the man said hastily.

'Yes, somehow that makes everything OK. What good is a "sorry" if it doesn't come after a solid knockout punch, right?' the Middler said, drily. 'How did you manage to snag this?' he nodded in the chariot's direction.

The man shrugged. 'The garage door was unlocked. Well, not really. I got one of those guardians to unlock it for me—delightful girls that lot, they've got the prettiest—Oh, hi,' he said, his eyes suddenly finding me. 'Who's this?'

'No one,' snapped the Middler. 'You won't find yourself in her future, so I don't see how it's any of your concern who she is.'

The Middler's tone puzzled me. What was it about this man that irked him so?

The man gave me a little smile. Something about his face reminded me of someone I'd seen on... what had it been? A card? A balloon? I couldn't quite place him, though I could've sworn I had seen him somewhere.

'Well, maybe later, then,' he winked, as if he knew something I, or indeed the Middler, didn't.

The Middler cleared his throat again. 'We'd better be off; important things to do.'

'I'll leave you to it, then,' said the man, brightly.

'Wonderful,' the Middler beckoned me to follow and we were off again.

I decided to let the smoke issuing from the Middler's nostrils dissipate before speaking up again.

'Who was that? What's his name?'

'Why do you want to know?'

'Curiosity!'

'Well, ignorance is bliss,' he snapped.

I gave him a long stare. 'What's *your* name?'

'Doesn't matter,' he said shortly.

'Why not?'

'You only need a name if you're going to become one.'

'Huh?'

'You won't understand, girl, just come along quietly. No more questions.'

I scowled. I had so many questions clamouring to be answered, and here he was, laying down ground rules for a walk between the clouds.

'How much longer?' I groaned, after we'd glided for what felt like an hour.

He shot me a sideways look. 'I believe we agreed on the No More Questions rule.'

'We didn't agree,' I rebutted. 'You said it, and I silently disregarded it.'

'We're nearly there,' he said brusquely.

The path narrowed to a small clearing, beyond which rose tall wrought-iron gates. The very look of those bars sent a chill down my body.

'Wait here,' the Middler instructed.

I had no problem obeying that particular order.

He hovered past the clearing, over to the gates, spoke something I couldn't hear, and traced a finger down a mighty padlock. There was a loud, echoing click, and the gates swung open, allowing a gush of wind to sweep towards where I stood.

'Come!' called the Middler.

I floated along silently, my sense of foreboding growing stronger every second. Past the gates, I could see a large garden. Tall trees stood swaying in the wind that seemed to blow in from nowhere at all. Flowers as large as bricks bloomed on the branches, but immediately withered away. Bright green leaves fell to the ground only to be sucked into muddy layers, only to be reborn on their branches once more. Melodious songs sounded in the distance before being replaced by terrifying war cries. The skies turned from clear blue to cloudy to stormy within seconds, on a loop. The unsettling sights and sounds were enough to send one into a mental spiral.

The Middler pointed at the garden. 'Go through these gates. Sit on the stool which appears in the middle of the brown grass, and wait.' His voice took on a more serious tone. 'Do not chew your fingernails, she doesn't like it. Do not blink too much, or he'll start yelling. And whatever you do, *please do not comment on his horns*.'

'His *what*?'

'Good luck, girl!'

And just like that, the Middler popped out of sight like a soap bubble in the air. Trying to remember all the instructions, I faced the gates, and with a deep sense of dread, entered the garden.

The minute I did, a patch of brown grass cropped up a few feet from me. Slowly, like a performer ascending a stage, a three-legged stool rose from underneath the ground. There was something intimidating about the way it stood there, like whilst on that stool, I'd make the most significant decision of my life. Well, afterlife (although it still hadn't sunk in).

I floated to the stool and perched myself on it.

For a long moment, nothing happened. I just sat there in the perturbing silence, waiting for something to happen. Anything to break the quiet.

And then, at long last, something did happen. A lone drop of rain fell from above, on the dry brown grass. Three more drops fell, and a few more, and a few more. It continued to drizzle until the patch of brown had turned a rich parrot green. Petrichor emanated from the ground, and I found myself transfixed by the smell of fresh earth.

Then, very abruptly, the earth turned dry again as the rain ceased to fall. Slowly, the winds changed. They became harsher, whistling differently, like they bore news of impending doom. There was something sinister about these winds, for they forced my thoughts in the direction of disaster and death and depression.

I saw things in my mind's eye—the smiles of innocents, the hostility of mobs. I heard voices, whispering sweet nothings and cunning lies.

Then, I began to feel it. A mixture of, well, everything—

joy, sorrow, clarity, confusion, exuberance, depression. Every emotion consumed me, making my head pound. I wanted to burst into song, but a chill filled my heart. My mind was embraced by a sense of calm, but almost immediately warped by terror.

I felt it all. Warmth to light up the heart, cold to chill the marrow; harps to free the soul, saws to scar the senses; hymns to clear the mind, curses to shatter the spirit. A confusing vortex of everything good and bad.

Without warning, the winds stopped howling, and my heart felt like it had been wiped clean of all emotion. My head stopped pounding. There was a sudden brightness that burst forth from everywhere, and I threw up an arm to shield my eyes. It was a whole minute before I could slowly lower my arm, and see, through the light my eyes were growing accustomed to, the two tall figures making their way towards me.

Surely, undoubtedly, unquestionably, I had to be dreaming. This was just too much.

2

The Decider

I shut my eyes firmly and reopened them, slowly.

Standing on the right was a woman. She was simply dazzling. I envied her large doe eyes, her intense gaze, and the confidence, wisdom and beauty which seemed to radiate out of her. Dark hair cascaded down her shoulders, braided elaborately with gold lace. Her silk sari was a delicate shade of honey, bringing out the colour in her eyes. As I gazed upon her form, I felt a calm wash over me, like I hadn't a worry in the world.

With great difficulty, I turned my attention to the man on the left—an inexpressibly good-looking man with a lazy smile stretching across chiselled features. He was dressed impeccably in a stark black suit. His shoes were shined bright like a mirror. His hair was swept back neatly, and there was an oddly enticing glint in his eyes. I found myself hopelessly drawn to them like a child to a chocolate.

'I am, as they say, devilishly handsome, aren't I?' grinned Satan, his voice as smooth as silk.

God rolled her eyes.

'Ignore him,' she said. 'His sense of humour has deteriorated ever since his horns began to grow inwards.'

Satan's hands immediately jumped to his hair, smoothing down two patches with a touch of nervousness.

'Blasted things,' he muttered to himself.

'Yes, what a pity,' drawled God. 'Anyway!' She clapped her hands with a sudden burst of vigour, 'Have you made your choice?' She looked at me expectantly.

I merely gawped at the two of them. Things were growing weirder and weirder by the minute.

I was in the presence of the two greatest forces in the world—God and Satan. If I recounted this experience to my friends, they'd send me packing to a psychotherapist, and not the cool type from the movies. I'm talking about dowdy old men in faded shirts, with offices that resemble a tool shed.

I was numb with disbelief. If this was still a dream, it was the longest one I'd ever had, not to mention the weirdest. And if it wasn't a dream, it could mean only one thing—I was going mad. All that Diet Coke I kept drinking; the fizz was finally destroying my brain cells and making me see things.

But then again, the two of them seemed so *real*. They seemed too solid to be cast off as figments of my imagination. That glow around them, the sheer power that seemed to pervade the garden, that wasn't imagined, surely?

I realised that I had wasted much time having these thoughts. I had to say something to God, so I opened my mouth to answer her, and said something super intelligent.

'Huglurgh.'

'Oh, goody,' said the Devil, 'we have a tubelight. How delightful.'

The insult barely hurt; Satan was so attractive, so charming, his voice was like...

'Snap out of it, girl!' God barked. She directly addressed the Devil. 'Enough with the dark enchantment! This is the Commons, it's against the rules to use your powers here!'

'You suck the fun out of everything,' complained the Devil. 'Fine! You! Zero-watt-brain, what's your choice?' he asked, pointing at me.

I pulled myself together as best as I could.

'My—my choice?'

'Yes, well, you *are* in the Choosing Commons,' God pointed out, waving an arm around the garden.

'I'm afraid, I don't understand you,' I said desperately.

They glanced at each other in exasperation. Then the Devil spoke.

'Did the Middler not tell you about your aura?'

'Evidently not,' God shook her head. 'I'll bet she hasn't even divined that she's dead. Arundathi, are you aware that you're dead?'

'To an extent.'

'And are you aware that you're now just a ghost?'

'Somewhat.'

'Are you aware that ghosts have auras?'

'What, like outlines?' I asked.

Satan cackled. It was the most unpleasant sound.

'Outlines! Oh, this girl is terrific!' He turned to God. 'You can keep her, I don't need someone this thick in my camp!'

'I scored 92 per cent in my twelfth boards,' I said stoutly.

Satan clapped slowly, his features reflecting mock-awe.

Rage overtook me. I wanted to snap his horns right off his head. The ground beneath the stool turned hot, and began to quake. Small columns of smoke rose around me, hissing and spitting like provoked serpents. For some reason, this seemed to please Satan, and his eyes shone with hunger.

God stepped in hurriedly.

'Congratulations on coming in twenty-third position in some random examination, Arundathi, but let's get back to more important things, shall we?'

I felt my anger abate slightly, and noticed the smoke dissolve into thin air.

'You were saying something... my aura...' I said, forcing myself to sound calm.

'Yes,' God said. 'Your aura is a reflection of your deeds, your actions, your conduct during your tenure as a mortal being. A predominantly red aura is indicative of a lot of wrongdoings, and buys you a one-way ticket to Hell, to join *his*...' she jerked her head in Satan's direction, 'forces. A predominantly golden aura says you've been exceptionally good, and allows you passage into Heaven, to join my forces.'

I frowned. 'So, why wasn't I ushered straight into Heaven or Hell? What am I still doing here?'

Satan scratched his chin.

'Wow, you can't operate outside a spectrum of stupidity, can you? Let me explain. You're a Halfling, someone with an undecided aura. Oh wait, I may need to break it down for you—it means you've done an equal amount of good and bad deeds during your stint on Earth.'

I blinked. 'So, I'm like that guy near the clouds? The Middler?'

'Ping ping ping ping ping!' Satan mimed a game show host. 'And she gets one right, ladies and gentlemen! That's right, sloth-face, you're half here, half there. So, before you unleash your question bank on us again, CHOOSE!'

The last word echoed across the Commons, leaving in its wake a deafening silence. I looked at God beseechingly.

'Satan, there is no need for surround sound.' Her voice was soft, but firm. 'Arundathi, look up.'

If I found her instruction confusing, I didn't let on. I did as she was told, and raised my head.

Above me was a glowing opaque circle of mingled red and gold. In a fit of childishness, I swatted at it, but it didn't fade. If anything, it glowed brighter still.

Beaten, I hung my head.

'As rowdy as Satan is, he is right,' God said to me. 'You must choose. Gold or red? Good or bad? Me or him?'

Satan tapped a foot impatiently. 'It's your call, pea-brain phantom.' He adjusted his cufflinks. 'Angel or Imp?'

❦

I sat on the stool, all numb. I felt like I was drowning in some void. I was chewing my fingernails nervously.

'Stop that!' snapped God, and I immediately desisted.

'Sorry, force of habit,' I mumbled. 'So, um, I have to make this choice between good and bad right now?'

'Nooo, no, take your time,' said Satan, his voice oozing sarcasm. 'It's not like I have villages to burn, banks to loot, Indian hockey to utterly destroy...'

'You just...' I started hotly, but God cut in.

'Actually, we're on a busy schedule. My avatar in Nepal just informed me that an old monk is stuck under an avalanche, so I have to help rescue him.'

'Ah, the avalanche happened, did it?' Satan smiled gleefully. 'I must rush back and give Frogspawn his promotion—he's doing some excellent work, and he's only a Level II imp!'

I was not paying attention to Satan.

'You have different avatars?'

'Obviously,' drawled Satan. 'The world is not just that

rat hole you call an apartment; it is indescribably huge. We create illusions of ourselves all over the planet. Human manifestations of our personalities, if you will... Just as well, can you imagine me without furs in Russia?'

I pictured Satan in a thick brown coat and a fluffy ushanka. Had the current circumstances been anything but deathly serious, I would've chuckled.

'So, you are the Indian avatar. But, then,' I said slowly, looking at Satan, 'why aren't you wearing a kurta or dhoti? What's with the suit?'

Satan looked smug. 'Ah, this little thing? It's Dolce. Do you get dhotis at Dolce? No? Didn't think so!'

God adjusted the folds on her sari. 'Time's wasting, Arundathi, make your decision. B or G?'

So that's what the Middler had meant earlier, I thought. B's and G's: bads and goods.

Satan cleared his throat. 'Just to help you make an informed decision, we have TVs in Hell, and we watch football every weekend. Support Manchester United, and you'll get prime seats next to the Lava Pit.'

A frown creased my forehead. 'Why Manchester United?'

'Duh, they're the red *devils*.'

Biting back an appropriate rejoinder, I turned to God.

'Um, your Almightiness, I am too bamboozled to make a decision. Actually,' I hesitated for a brief second, 'I'm not entirely sure this is even happening. It seems like I'm dead, and my appearance also indicates that, but it's not sinking in.'

The two powers sighed in unison.

'Come here.' Satan ordered. He snapped his long fingers and an iPad appeared in his hand. 'Check this out.'

It was a video uploaded on a website called gruesomedeathvistas.com. I stared at the morbid name.

'Creative, isn't it?' chortled Satan. 'Came up with it myself, thank you very much.'

The video was hazy, but the elements were perceivable. There I was, hustling down the station, my ponytail swinging from side to side. My friends' voices echoed in the night. I was standing on the railway lines like a deer caught in headlights before WHAM! I was mowed down by the train. If the horrible crash hadn't completely atomized me, the multiple wheels riding over my body definitely had.

As my friends let out terrible screams, I saw something else. Something was escaping my body—several wisps of pale white vapour. They rose slowly from the broken remains of my body, like fumes from the ruins of a smouldering wreckage, and ascended high above the railway tracks before coming together to form a white shape. A human shape. *My* ghost...

The video blurred, and there was nothing left to see or hear but the white noise.

I stared at the screen with my eyes out of focus until Satan's voice penetrated my ears.

'OI!' he thundered. 'Heard a word of what I said?'

I gave him a glum look.

'That's all the evidence you need of your death, girl,' snapped Satan, now sounding very impatient indeed. 'And we've wasted enough time here. You have,' he checked his watch, 'eight minutes and forty-seven seconds to make a decision. I have a very urgent order to give to the Department of Feline Roadkill.'

God gagged. 'Do you have to be so nasty in front of her?'

'Yeah, well, it was in my job description,' Satan pointed out.

'Arundathi, that *is* all the time we can give you,' said God, not unkindly. 'For better or for worse, you will have to make a choice. You have eight minutes. Decide.'

I looked down at the ground, my thoughts flitting about haphazardly in my mind.

So I really was dead. One hundred per cent, irrevocably dead. Clarity pierced my doubt-ridden brain like a bullet. I wasn't dreaming, after all. I'd strayed right into a nightmare. I'd stormed away from my friends, away from life itself, and into the cold clammy embrace of death. If only I'd listened to my friends, heard the sincerity in their pleading voices... if only I could turn back the hands of time... I wouldn't be standing here. I wouldn't be dead.

Before I knew what was happening, I was drawing short, sharp breaths. Tears filled my eyes and coursed down my cheeks. Soon, I was sobbing uncontrollably. I wasn't going back to where I came from. I would never grow old.

I'd left everything behind—my friends, my grandmother, my half-finished book, my photographs, my stamp collection, my diary heavy with secrets, my grandfather's old watch, my shoe cabinet where I'd hidden articles I'd never send to magazines, my mixed CDs which had been gifts from a favourite cousin—I would never get them back. I would never get my life back.

The harsh reality of my situation crashed into me harder than the train, and fresh tears splashed onto my lap only to be absorbed into the silvery jeans.

'Time's up!' Satan's voice called from a million kilometres away. 'And the afterlife-altering decision is?'

I looked up at God and Satan with swollen eyes.

'I don't know,' I said in a small voice.

'I beg your pardon?' hissed Satan.

'I don't know,' I repeated, my voice growing stronger. 'I'm *dead*. I'm a ghost of my former self, literally! I will never lie on my grandmother's lap again, I will never hi-five Shirley again, I will never wear my favourite sweatshirt again. I am trying to come to terms with the fact that I am looking at an eternity without anything I held dear. So, no, I don't know what to choose. There.'

Satan looked highly affronted. 'See what happens when we're lenient with them?' he spat at God. 'If it hadn't been for your bloody *Commons* rubbish, I'd have already recruited this idiot; my infantry division is pitiful!' He paused. 'Better yet, I could've turned her into a nice foot rug!'

God considered me for a moment. 'She does seem to be more resilient than the average ghost.'

'Resilient?' Satan arched his eyebrows. '*Resilient?* I think the word you're looking for is "impudent"!'

'Oh, but that should please you, though, shouldn't it?' God was quick to point out. 'It does, after all, have "imp" in it.'

Satan could only glare at God.

'Speechlessness. Wow, a first from you.' She motioned in my direction. 'What do we do now?'

'I suggest we burn her,' said Satan, in a bored voice. 'I just need to text the Department of Spirit Scorching.' He produced a sleek phone from an inside pocket and began to type a message. 'They've not had anything to look forward to since I called off the Boy Band Extermination Programme.'

'There will be no talk of burning Arundathi.' God snatched the phone away from Satan, who made a noise like an injured puppy. 'That sort of action is beyond the pale! And just imagine the amount of paperwork!'

'Are you saying we just let her hover here in the Commons for bloody eternity? I won't tolerate such a weak verdict, it sickens me,' said Satan. 'The idiot has to choose to belong somewhere.'

God steepled her fingers and thought for a few moments while Satan casually sparked and put out flames on the tips of his fingers, his eyes boring into me. It was very disturbing.

Then, God smiled in a very odd way, like she'd come up with something very, very mischievous.

'Maybe it's time to bring out the Checklist.'

Satan looked as though he had been smacked in the face by an errant snowball.

'Are. You. Joking?' he growled, his voice growing louder with every word. 'No way in Hell will I let that happen!'

'Why not?' asked God, the flame of excitement lighting up her eyes. 'We've never done it before, and here is a case that's presented itself so wonderfully.'

Satan looked ready to spit fire at anyone in his vicinity.

'Look, woman, I'm not prepared to bargain for a ghost that belongs just as much to me as she does to you. The Checklist is unfair, it's designed to make you win!'

'How so?'

'The tasks are unevenly divided!'

'I cannot be held responsible for your mistakes. You defaulted on the number of tasks when we set them.'

'I WAS OTHERWISE OCCUPIED!' Satan bellowed. 'I WAS BUSY UPROOTING THE EGYPTIAN CIVILIZATION!'

The spittle passed right through me.

'Um,' I ventured. 'Not to interrupt your friendly conversation, but, what in blazes are you talking about?'

The two powers glowered at me, obviously displeased by

a puny ghost interrupting their umpteenth argument.

'There's another way to determine your fate,' said God shortly. 'It's called the Checklist.'

'Or as I call it, the Dung-log,' Satan drawled.

God ignored him. 'It enumerates a specific number of tasks a ghost should complete before he or she returns to the Choosing Commons to be taken on as an Imp or an Angel.'

For the first time since dying, a spark of hope ignited inside me.

'That sounds fair!'

'Fair, my spiky tail!' cried Satan.

'How is it not?' countered God.

'The girl will choose to do good!'

'Not necessarily, look at her aura.'

Satan cast around for another counterpoint, and seemed to find one. A horribly weak one.

'The list contains five tasks—three good and two bad. That's not even equal!'

'So add one more of yours *now*,' suggested God.

'I…hmmm.' Satan looked at God with newfound admiration. 'Why didn't I think of that?'

'Because you have stale oatmeal for brains, that's why,' said God with resounding finality.

I suppressed a giggle.

Satan straightened his tie. 'It appears I have no choice. Let's get to the Checklist, shall we?' He turned to God, who produced a scroll with a lazy wave of her hand.

'*Thirteen Ways to Convert a Manchester United suppor...* oops, wrong scroll,' she laughed sheepishly. 'Ah, here it is. *The Checklist—To be employed in case of lack of ghostly defeatism*.'

She cleared her throat importantly, and started reading out the scroll—

'*According to Article 661(S) Clause Intervention, Sub-Clause The-Spirits-be-damned* (really now, Satan!), *in the event that a ghost(s) is found to be unwavering in their intent to miff the hair off your head*—I told you not to tamper with the list!!—*we, the two reigning powers of Good and Evil—God and Satan—will find it within our capacity to invoke the Checklist, thereby subjecting the spirit(s) in question to a series of predetermined and dealterable*—use that dictionary I chucked at you last year, Satan—*tasks*.'

I waited with bated breath, but further instruction did not seem forthcoming.

'Well?' I prompted. 'What are the tasks?'

God didn't say anything. She merely rolled up the scroll, walked down to me and dropped it into the front pocket of my jeans. Surprisingly, it didn't fall right through. It just clung to my pocket like it had some dark or divine power, which, I reminded myself, it probably did.

'The tasks will appear to you when you return to Earth,' she said.

I deflated. 'That's unfair! What if I read them and discover I'm not prepared?'

'Balderdash,' Satan said, casually waving a hand. 'You weren't given time to prepare for death, and you seem to be coping with it just fine now.'

Two pairs of eyes bore into Satan's cold black ones.

'That's nice,' God said sarcastically. 'Really sensitive.'

'They don't call me Mr Sympathetic for nothing.' Saying so, the Lord of Darkness took a dramatic bow.

I drew in a great shuddering breath and glanced at God. 'Once I complete these tasks, I get back here and join either you or Satan?'

'Yeah, it's like when they form sports teams, except this time, *you'll* actually get picked by one, Spectre the Scrawny,' Satan said, sniggering.

I didn't take Satan's bait; the last time I'd given in to anger, I'd walked right into the path of a speeding train. Anger, obviously, was bad news. It would make my aura redder, and that would render the Checklist unnecessary, and I'd find myself stuck in the company of the Devil in Dolce for eternity.

God stepped back and stood in line with Satan.

'You have three days to complete six tasks,' she declared. 'The minute your feet touch the Earth, your countdown will start. When the final task is done, you will be pulled back here. You will return to this garden even if your tasks remain unchecked on that list.'

'Yeah, in which case we get to burn you,' smiled Satan.

This time, God didn't snub him. I wondered if she was exasperated or if she agreed with him.

'Any questions?' she asked.

'No,' I said, resignedly.

'Good luck!' said Satan, grinning wickedly. 'I look forward to overseeing your combustion.'

'Do me proud, Arundathi,' said God quietly.

Their forms began to blur. I assumed that soon they would pull that trick most omnipotent beings do on telly, and turn into a ball of energy that would blind me. But they didn't, they merely grew smaller in size, as if reversing into a very brightly lit tunnel.

'Wait!' I called desperately after their retreating forms. Something had suddenly struck me. 'Don't I get any help with these tasks? An Imp or Angel to advise me? Anything?'

Satan smirked and reached into an inner pocket of his suit. He pulled out a thin booklet, predictably bound in leather as black as Satan's merciless eyes. Without warning, he chucked it at me: *Hell's Hacks for the Hapless Soul*. I flipped through the booklet. Words like 'Perfect Possession' and '21 Ways to Animate the Inanimate' leapt out of the pages.

'What's this?' I asked.

'Help,' said Satan. 'Looks like you'll be needing lots of it.'

I looked doubtfully from the booklet to Satan, and then to God.

God looked at me with a sad, almost doleful look in her eyes.

'All the help you need is within you. The Angel lives inside your person. You have listened to her thus far, she will continue to guide you now.'

And with that, both of them turned away. I blinked, and they were gone.

The next second, the garden disappeared, the stool vanished, and I was lifted into the air and tossed backwards along the path and outside the gate.

3

A Colourful Return

'You're back, I see,' the Middler observed, as I hit a cloud with a soft 'flump'

'You weren't expecting me, were you?' I brushed bits of cloud off myself and glanced at him. 'Where's your clipboard?'

'Gone,' sighed the Middler. 'No deaths, no lists. Although the same can't be said for you,' he bobbed his head at the scroll in my jeans. 'They Checklist-ed you, eh?'

'How do you know about the list?' I asked in amazement.

'I've spent fifteen millennia around here, missy. There's not much that gets past me.'

'Fifteen millennia?' I whistled. 'That sounds like hell.'

'The Void actually, remember?' He laughed bitterly. He caught my pitying expression and rearranged his face to its normal, arrogant self. 'So, you have to get back down now! Excited?'

'Kind of nervous,' I admitted.

'Don't worry. You'll do just fine.'

We started to float away from the Void and towards the low-hanging clouds.

'Got any tips for me?' I asked.

'Sure, here's a rupee,' the Middler placed an old coin in my hand.

I gave him a stony look, even as the coin fell through my palm and disappeared into the cloud.

'You've got no sense of humour,' he lamented. 'Fine, if it's aid you need, it's aid you shall get.' He rummaged through a knapsack, which I had not noticed earlier.

'Here.' He slipped a chain into my hand. It was a long string of silver, with a curious pendant dangling from it—a pair of horns sprouting from a halo.

'Wow, whose is this?' I asked, admiring the necklace. It didn't fall from my hands.

'Mine,' the Middler said simply.

'And why're you giving it to me?' I asked him suspiciously.

'Do you want help or not?'

'Sorry,' I said hastily. 'So, apart from a fashion accessory, what is this thing?'

'It will help you with your tasks,' explained the Middler. 'Wear it around your neck and you'll become visible only to the person you wish to.'

'Why would I want to be seen?' I couldn't think of any reason except spooking the living daylights out of Rishi.

'You just might want to be *seen*, believe me,' said the Middler, but didn't give any further explanation.

'What happens if I take it off?' I asked, pocketing it.

The Middler shrugged his shoulders. 'You're a ghost to everyone once more; as invisible as the eleventh player in a batting line-up.'

'Hey, you're a cricket fan!'

'I do enjoy the occasional boundary,' said the Middler. 'Especially as I am in a place devoid of one,' he added, more to himself than to me.

There was a short pause and then I glanced at my aura.

'You knew, didn't you? You knew I wouldn't be able to decide for myself in the Choosing Commons.'

'From the minute you zoomed into my office, yes,' said the Middler, shrewdly.

'How?'

The Middler's eyes flicked to my aura. 'Your aura is perfectly split. I haven't seen something like this in so many millennia. Someone who's so disputed, so confused about their intentions and actions, such a person cannot make an instantaneous, permanent decision, now, can they?'

I blinked. 'I'm not that confused, am I?'

'You tell me,' he said softly. 'You were in that garden. You saw happiness and sorrow, peace and war, light and darkness. You saw the best of times, you saw the worst of times. And yet, you couldn't place yourself anywhere, you didn't know where you belonged. You felt an invisible force pull you from *both* sides of the path. You're divided all the time, perpetually incurring your own confusion. You don't even know who you are.'

My eyes misted, but I blinked the tears away.

'What time will it be when I get back on Earth? How long have I been up here?'

'You'll reach Bangalore in an hour,' said the Middler, looking at a Victorian-style pocket watch. 'So, say around half past nine.'

'What?' I yelped. 'I died at midnight! I've been here for eight hours?'

'You took long to get here, but I don't blame you.' The Middler's face mirrored frustration. 'The Phantom Highway was clogged.'

'Er, what?'

The Middler waved an impatient hand. 'Souls tend to wander around unconsciously before flying into the highway and after that they're stuck on it.' The anger in his voice grew. 'It'd be fine if that complete idiot Kotumai managed the traffic better. It's not even like he has outgoing traffic! He's become incorrigible ever since Satan gave him a small crown, thinks he owns the bloody highway.'

'Kotumai?' I asked, trying to make sense of this gibberish.

'Oh, he's an Imp now,' said the Middler. 'Used to be a traffic policeman; he died on the job and he's been looking for the idiot who ran him over ever since.'

'Right,' I said vaguely. 'Anyway, about these tasks—how do I complete them? I can barely hold a pencil without letting it fall right through.'

'You're not unintelligent,' replied the Middler. 'You'll figure it out.'

I didn't feel altogether reassured. The Middler stepped closer to me.

'Look, it is not my place to offer much help. As to how you will manage the Checklist, that's your responsibility, isn't it? But here's a word of warning: Beware. Of everything. There is more to fear on Earth than there is in Hell, believe me, I know. I've seen awful things from up here. Evil is omnipresent, and can lurk as much in sunshine as it can in the darkest of night. Evil will find you when you least expect it, and use your deepest fears and darkest thoughts against you. Malice, hatred...they can and will try to find you, and if and when then do, you have to strengthen your defences against them.' He straightened. 'Fortunately, there is some good, too. Kindness, sympathy...they're your allies. They'll answer your call if you find the compassion to help someone. Remember, there is no darkness so solid that a small spark cannot break. Find it, and use it well.'

I made to smile and thank him for his help, but my lips could just about manage a grimace. We'd reached the lowest cloud.

It ended a few feet away from us, and beyond its dull lining, the blue skies stretched like a seamless blanket.

My nervousness was palpable. The Middler said, 'Need some help?'

'A little,' I squeaked.

'Ready?'

'Yeah,' I replied, feeling anything but ready.

'Great! See you soon, Arundathi Jayaram!'

He gave me a push and I stumbled forward into a patch of clear blue sky. For a second, I simply hovered there. From there on, it was a free fall for me.

In an instant, the wind lifted my hair and hoisted the strands over my head where they danced like giant black flames. Instinctively, I raised my hands, my palms open and imploring, hoping that somehow the clouds would pull me back up. But, no. I was a skydiver without a parachute. I pulled off a series of somersaults without meaning to. It wasn't hard, what with the wind tossing me this way and that like a leaf in a storm.

I wasn't afraid of heights, but that didn't stop me from screaming. The sound of the wind and the sight of my ghostly end gave me the creeps.

I didn't know what lay in store for me back on Earth. I didn't know how I'd feel roaming the streets and looking at all those solid, alive people. I didn't know what to expect. So, I shut my eyes, began to count backwards from one hundred, and waited for the sound of Bangalore around me.

❦

I opened my eyes after some time and realized that I was now lost in a sea of dark grey clouds.

I'd definitely plummeted a good ten thousand feet without any major episode. Knowing me, the flying start to my afterlife was too good to last. After all, no self-respecting plummeting incident is ever twist-free. Especially if said plummeting incident involved someone like me. I was a beacon for disasters, even in my afterlife.

Things were spiralling out of control, I caught the sight of the Earth below me, but I couldn't control myself. I slowed down the same way a hydroplaning car does—I had no brakes.

Gravity was being slightly unfair in the way it was functioning here. Frankly, I thought it had a bit of an attitude problem. Either that or it was exacting revenge on me. I obviously didn't care for Physics much, so now Physics had decided to fail me!

Shrieking like a banshee on fire, I fell, spinning like a top, and becoming more and more disoriented with every kilometre I put behind me.

I felt myself slowing down, but the world around me was still not solid earth. I wasn't in Bangalore yet, but I was nearing it, as it had started to drizzle unpredictably. It dawned on me that it was the sudden arrival of all the nimbus clouds that made me a whirlpool-impersonation.

When I became steady, and started descending with a touch of grace, I took it all in.

The drops of rain looked like pearls. I felt like a child again, sticking my tongue out and trying to catch the water with my fingertips. If the sun was making an effort to conceal itself, it was doing a pretty poor job, hiding behind clouds for only a few seconds. Its rays, like buttery-golden ribbons, shone through the dark clouds beautifully.

But my pleasant smile of surprise morphed seamlessly into an expression of astonishment as I noticed something strange—someone was making her way out of the large grey clouds, on a rainbow, which appeared as she walked.

The boots—brilliant violet and shiny—stuck out first. Indigo stockings, a blue skirt and a green belt registered themselves in quick succession. I didn't see anything wrong with the yellow blouse, but the dazzling orange face and flaming red hair were painfully conspicuous in that they were, well, dazzling orange and flaming red.

As she stepped out of the cloud, a couple of Angels (they appeared to be, at least, in their white dresses and shiny halos) nearby yelped in shock and flew off to an unpopulated cloud, muttering about the dangers of polychromatic women.

'It's rude to stare, you know,' she said to me.

She enunciated every word, like she was on stage and I was her audience.

'I'm sorry,' I said, as I finally stopped in front of her, falling right beside her on the rainbow. 'I was just startled, that's all.'

'Startled? Hmmm,' she said with a deep frown. 'Most people are pleasantly surprised to see me.'

'Oh, yeah,' I said, nodding. 'Those two Angels looked mighty happy with your arrival.'

'Sarcasm does not become you, Spirit,' said the woman, shrugging and bringing her blouse to rest on her shoulders properly.

'No, but it did keep my blood pressure steady some time ago.' I replied. 'So, um, who are you?'

'I thought it was evident from my flamboyant garb,' said the woman, as she ran her fingers through her hair. 'I am Vibgyor the Rainbow. But you can call me V.'

❦

V's perfume was so strong, it was a wonder I didn't faint from the smell. I couldn't see myself, obviously, but I knew my expression was the same it had been when my grandmother had introduced my taste buds to soy milk.

We were gliding along the sky, which was the best experience I'd had so far. It was sunny, and yet, raindrops were falling fast and thick. The IT city was visible below me now, but we were still way above the Earth. The apartments were specks and the roads running between them were thin lines.

With every step V took, a bit of rainbow stretched

across the sky. Colourful bricks of red, green, blue and four other shades manifested themselves in front of us, creating a pathway along which we could go. It was a sight I'd never forget.

I looked at V's colourful form and felt stunned by her appearance all over again. I could've asked her a million things, and yet I started with—

'Hey, so, do you suffer from carotenosis?'

'No,' V said simply. 'Why do you ask?' she added, absently scratching her orange jaw.

'Oh, um, no reason.' I looked away.

The rain had quietened to a soft but steady pour, leaving our surroundings grey and blurred, and every time the sun dived behind clouds, V would become a hazy mix of colours, which was slightly amusing. It was like mixing paints in a palette.

I caught a whiff of V's perfume again.

'You know, I really love rainbows,' I said brightly.

'Yes?'

'Especially when they are doused in perfume.'

V had the grace to blush. Or something to that effect; you couldn't really tell with that much orange on your cheeks.

'Apologies, Spirit,' she said.

'Arundathi.'

'Hmmm?'

'Arundathi,' I repeated. 'That's my name. You don't have

to call me Spirit.'

'Ah, right, of course,' she said, bobbing her head. 'Arundathi. Bit of an odd name, isn't it?'

'Well, *Vibgyor*, what can I say?' I smiled. 'Anyway, what's with the excessive perfume? Massive discount on Chanel?'

'If you must know,' said V, a little testily, 'my shower broke this morning.'

'Right,' I nodded. 'I mean, it's not like you're a rainbow, and you can come out when it's raining and there's plenty of water around. Oh, wait...'

V adopted a dignified silence, which was filled with the appearance of a few more colourful bricks.

'So, do you like rainbows?' she asked.

'Everyone likes rainbows!' I said, laughing slightly.

'Always nice to hear!' chimed V. 'And what is it about my work that you find enjoyable?'

'Well,' I said slowly. 'You're so colourful, for one.'

'My personality does shine through, yes,' V said, sounding very matter-of-fact about it.

'And you lighten the mood if things are tense. You're like a happy potion, you know?'

'Now, now, you don't have to flatter me,' said V, trying not to look too smug.

'And here's the best part,' I said. 'Once, I took a picture of a rainbow from my terrace, and put it up on Instagram, and it got some hundred Likes. Best post of mine so far!'

V's palm made contact with her forehead so fast, it was a blur of colours.

'What?' I asked indignantly.

'Nothing, nothing,' said V, shaking her head and sighing dramatically. 'I just liked the nineteenth century a lot better, that's all. We didn't have social media then. What a blessed time it was.'

'Er, didn't the blessed time also have the eruption of the Krakatoa volcano?'

'Yes, it did,' snapped V. 'And a good thing, too, that it happened back then, because had it happened today, all you would've done is put it up on Instaglam.'

'Instagram,' I corrected her.

'Oh lord, sorry. Forgive me for that transgression!' she cried, clapping her hands over her face in a very theatrical gesture.

Somehow, miraculously, I'd ticked off another magical being, and her annoyance was a visual spectacle; the yellow bricks were turning brown, and her yellow blouse was becoming khaki.

Damage control! Damage control! yelped my inner voice.

'I love your shoes.'

'Thanks,' said V, rather stiffly.

'Are they Italian?'

V scoffed. 'Please, like Italians know anything about shoe-making.'

I bit my tongue and let her talk.

'I got my shoes tailored by The Cobbler himself.'

'Like... guys who sit at street corners and stitch up torn soles?' I asked, surprised. 'Do we still have a lot of them left?'

'Not cobblers in general, Arundathi,' said V, with strained patience. '*The* Cobbler! The very first cobbler in the world. He fashioned a shoe out of marigolds and moonbeams, they say. And when the man he sold it to walked, he illuminated the world around him, and left golden flowers in his wake.'

'Woah!' I said, stunned. But V seemed to know that I was judging her.

She said, 'It is people like you, Arundathi, who encourage shoe snobbery. When supermodels wear the acid green shoes, you'll worship the ground the shoes walked on.'

I was about to argue with her, but realised there was too much truth in her words. She had a point—the leopard print had very possibly been regarded as an eyesore before it became an iconic print just because someone walking the ramp had flaunted it. Why else would anyone want to look like a spotted, humanoid cat?

'So,' I ventured after a while, 'is it mandatory for you to dress like this or is it personal choice?'

'What are you getting at?' V snapped.

I threw up my hands defensively. 'Hey, just an innocent question! You don't see a lot of people going around looking like a gift wrapping station, that's all!'

'Oh, that's lovely,' said V scathingly. 'You should be a… a… a fashion blogger.'

'I could, but my bank balance would weep.'

Silence buzzed between us again, and it was noisier than actual sound.

'So, um, about your dress?'

V breathed deeply. 'I was born this way. Everything about me is unchangeable. And I am thrilled that is so, because I love being a performer, and this attire goes with the image.'

'A performer? Really?' I giggled involuntarily. For some reason, all I could think of were trapeze artists, which immediately made me think of clowns.

V looked affronted. 'And what about being a performer causes you to chortle?'

'Nothing, it's just…' I cast around for the right words, 'I don't know… flashy.'

V drew herself up to her full height. 'There is nothing *flashy* about showmanship! It is not glamour and glitz alone that is sought! Showmanship transcends all that! It is about a love for drama, for the expressive and evocative art form. It is a love for enthralling and entertaining, even if only for a few seconds! And the appreciation that follows, if any, is what a showman revels in. That feeling of elation is second to nothing!'

I felt slightly abashed. 'Sorry, sorry, I didn't really get it, that's all. I meant no offence.'

V looked slightly mollified. 'Well, alright then.'

'Tell me something,' I said after some time. 'How come you never visit Bangalore anymore? We see you so rarely down there.'

V smirked, with seven colours gleaming from between her lips.

'You people…pah! You wouldn't appreciate a performance!' she snarled. 'You are too busy to look up from your computers. You wouldn't recognize a rainbow unless it entered your homes dressed as a start-up.'

'Hey!' I whined in protest.

'Tell me I'm wrong,' spat V. 'I hung around for an entire afternoon last month. The only person to take any notice of me was an old beggar weeping into his ragged shirt. He looked up, saw me, and a smile shone through his tears. He actually folded his palms up to the sky. Sadly, I haven't seen the old man for some time now. Maybe they've shut down Cubbon Park, so he's left its green cove now. With the poor fellow gone, I can cut short my Bangalore plans to once, maybe twice a year.'

'Can you even see people from up here?' I whistled, completely missing the point.

V merely shook her head and walked on, muttering to herself. Every few steps, I caught the words 'no appreciation' and 'start-ups'.

We reached my city before I knew it. I saw the rooftops

of some very familiar buildings, and caught myself smiling fondly at them. I could hear the ominous sounds of rush hour pretty much everywhere.

In no time at all, we'd reached the end of the rainbow on top of a multistorey building. The pathway curved downwards now, and it was time to say goodbye to V.

She was glaring in the opposite direction, apparently frustrated to be back in a place that didn't value her enough. I shifted uncomfortably, scratching my neck and looking awkward.

'Thank you for the journey, it was really nice,' I said, although I didn't really mean it. I couldn't recall a single journey that had been as weird, albeit extraordinary, as this.

V shrugged. 'Yes, well, goodbye and all that.'

'I'll think of you every time it rains,' I said, attempting a smile.

V rolled her eyes.

'No, really!' I said hastily. 'And I won't even consider Instagram.'

'What about all those precious Likes?'

I waved off the suggestion airily. 'Oh, who cares? I'll just … Enjoy the blessed nineteenth century.'

Grudgingly, it seemed, V laughed. 'You won't forget me?' she asked a little childishly.

It will be years before I forget that perfume, to be honest, I thought to myself.

'Of course not,' I heard myself say. 'I'll even keep an eye out for the old man in Cubbon Park. I'll try and send you a wish from him, I promise. You know, for an encore from you.'

V gave me a grudging smile. 'That would be nice.'

We exchanged a handshake, and then, with a tiny wave, I stepped off the colourful rainbow road. Out of the corner of my eye, I saw V popping out of sight, taking her spectrum with her.

I rubbed my hands and looked around, glad to be back in the city that held my past. In an instant, I knew exactly where I was.

The Silk Board junction on a Monday morning was absolute chaos.

4
First Task

The signal was broken. Cars, buses, autorickshaws and motorbikes were threatening to tear out each other's bumpers, and pedestrians crossed the street like headless chickens. The pavements were fenced with refuse from the night before, and sweepers in tattered uniforms swept its corners, throwing up puffs of dust. Horns blared from every corner of the road. A young biker roared along from a narrow path to skip the traffic signal's red light, while an autorickshaw overtook him, the car driver yelling something about wasted licences.

The only thing more useless that the 'One Way' sign on the road was the lone policeman in the corner, who was too busy adjusting the belt buckle under his potbelly to pay much attention to the city's utter disregard for rules.

I stared in dismay. For a second, I wondered if I was in real Hell.

I sat cross-legged on the roof of the building and took

a deep breath. My mind raced over the events which had occurred within the span of a day.

No weirder things had happened before.

I felt around in my jeans and took out the booklet Satan had been so kind as to throw at me. I flipped it open and skimmed its contents, looking for something, anything, that looked likely to help me at this point.

A chapter caught my eye, and I began to read.

Spirits are bound by the ancient laws of the Greater Worlds, namely, Heaven and Hell. As such, their powers are linked to both the privileges as well as restrictions of the Worlds. While the bane of their existence is the absence of a body in which to permanently reside, spirits can temporarily inhabit that which they wish to, be it humans or objects at various levels of inanimateness. However, it wasn't until the birth of the third century that spirits actually found themselves capable of the astonishing power of Possession. Indeed, it was the ghost of Rabila the Eleventh from modern-day Malaysia, who, in her eagerness to get out of a smelly bathroom, found herself locked inside the body of the flush tank for thirty-five minutes before realizing she had inadvertently discovered this strange power.

I snapped the booklet shut and shook myself mentally, remembering that I had a timetable to adhere to. I reached for the Checklist and smoothed it open.

The sandy parchment was blank. And for a long moment, it stayed that way. I scratched the parchment, flicked it smartly with my fingertips and, feeling silly, tried talking to it, but to no avail. I was just considering crumpling it up when something happened.

Tiny golden letters appeared on its rough surface in an elegant slanted handwriting. As they curved and twisted, I felt nervous anticipation stir and form sweat on my forehead.

Thou shalt help a complete stranger.

After a very pregnant pause, I laughed out loud in relief. That seemed absurdly simplistic! I was in a metropolis where every third person needed help with something—changing a flat tyre, moving an uprooted tree, widening their vocabulary to curse the roads and rain that had caused the tyre to flatten and the tree to uproot itself...

I tucked away the list and straightened up.

A boy in baggy jeans crossed my building, and a one-armed beggar tried to pry coin from him. Maybe I could help the old man? No, I wasn't exactly liquid myself, now or ever.

And then I saw her—a girl on a red scooter. The vehicle sounded as though it was having a serious case of Monday morning blues. It whined, protested, made distasteful gurgling noises. It did everything but start. Passers-by took little or no notice of the girl's problem; it was as if she wasn't there.

I had found the subject of my first task.

Allowing myself to pass cleanly through the roof of the building and its bolted front door, I flew out into the open once more.

The girl took her helmet off. She was pretty, I observed, with an oval face and shiny, black hair which she'd pulled back into a fashionably clumsy bun. She was petite, dressed in a pair of jeans and a T-shirt which was a mess of colours; pink, green and yellow splashed across her chest with a smiley saying, 'Cheers!' I found that ironic given her current situation.

Sitting down on the pavement, I amused myself for a few moments while she kicked and shook the scooter, calling it all sorts of names her parents would've disapproved of. By the time she'd exhausted her supply of expletives, her palms were pink and sweaty, and her jeans were coated with mud and slush.

I rubbed my palms, all set to lend a helpful hand. Then I froze.

How exactly was I going to fish this girl out of troubled waters? She couldn't see me or talk to me. My fingers would pass as uselessly through her as Trigonometry did through my brain. I needed a medium, some way to channel my help.

It was a full minute before I remembered what I'd read in the booklet. I was a ghost. And one of the perks of being one was the simple yet effective power of Possession. I could turn any person, object or animal into my place of residence.

Congratulating myself on what I chose to call cool logic in a trying situation, I started looking for a body with a gentle soul to possess.

The guy with the tattoos wouldn't do; I didn't want to

mess with any soul which permitted its owner to puncture their forearms like that. Besides, his very appearance would freak the girl out. Something about the obnoxious look on the woman passing me by told me she wouldn't yank a one-legged puppy from the jaws of death if it meant she'd have to lift a finger. And the paan-chewing bus driver? Definitely not. I craned my neck, and then I spotted him.

'Ah.' My face spit into a wide grin.

I recognized him instantly. He was behind the wheel of a big car—Giridhar, my neighbour Meera Aunty's husband.

A receding hairline, mid-thirties, ID card around his neck, and a sunken look in his eyes suggestive of a sapped soul—Giridhar was the textbook definition of a corporate stooge. He was the perfect candidate for my first Possession.

Here we go, I thought, and dived headlong into the man's body. It was bedlam.

The instant I took possession of this man, a boisterous part of his soul rejected me. This man would make a belligerent ghost, I thought. While I fought with the irritating soul, all my thoughts became mingled with his. I was suddenly bombarded with a mishmash of reminders about mango cheesecakes and an upcoming performance appraisal, the smell of old books and an upcoming performance appraisal, acne cream and an upcoming performance appraisal. There was also the matter of blending into this man—it was highly off-putting. His capacious stomach was obviously a result of one too many samosas.

After much tussling with the soul fragment, I took total control of this man. 'Alright, Mr G, let's help a young lady today.' I heard the words escape Giridhar's lips in a dull voice.

I directed him to steer the car to the left, parking it a few feet behind the girl with the hiccupping scooter.

'Excuse me, may I help you?'

The girl stopped roughing her scooter and looked at me. She was sweating profusely and her eye make-up was ruined. I noticed the wary look she threw my way, before finally giving in and admitting, 'Yeah, my scooter won't start!'

I lumbered forward, not accustomed to this much bulk near my waistline.

The scooter was covered from headlight to taillight in mud and muck. I wrinkled my nose.

'Did you try kick-starting it?'

'Several times,' nodded the girl.

'Hmmm.'

I took a good look at the kick-start, stand, seat and a funny little flap near the taillight before I came to a conclusion: I knew *nothing* about scooters.

'Maybe you should call the nearest service centre?' I suggested.

The girl made an impatient noise. 'I did that already. They said they would take an hour to get here. An hour! Can you imagine?'

Given the rocky relationship that Bangalore's roads shared with traffic and most forms of precipitation, I imagined it could've been a lot worse. I smiled lamely, not knowing what else to do. My mind had turned blank, like a slate wiped clean. I just stood there gawping at her.

'Ok, um, thanks anyway,' said the girl suddenly, taking a step backwards.

It occurred to me that a thirty-something man staring at a young girl was exceedingly creepy. A stupid, apologetic smile tugged at the corners of my lips.

'Sorry, I was just thinking,' I improvised.

I forced myself to do what I had told the girl I was doing. Finally, an idea flashed to life in my mind. I entered a part of Giridhar's brain which stored old memories. There were all sorts of things in there—he was a pimply kid riding a bike; he was on a trek with his parents; a pellet hit him in the back of his head inside a classroom; he was squatting in a small parking lot with a rusty old—scooty! I thought to myself triumphantly. With a rush of energy, I plunged into all his ideas and thoughts of his old two-wheeler. Immediately, like a TV commercial, images flashed to life. Cylinders, chokes and carburettors. Giridhar's generous brain threw up fact after fact about the inner workings of a scooty, and I caught them all for fear of getting stuck inside a choke for the rest of my afterlife. I had to give it to Giridhar—this guy was an encyclopaedia!

I turned to the girl.

'Has it been long since you have driven this scooty before today?'

'Um, yeah,' the girl bit her lip, 'maybe a few months.'

I nodded and smiled knowingly. 'Give me a few minutes.'

Rolling up my sleeves, I squatted with a groan and squinted at the scooter. Using Giridhar's collection of memories, I fidgeted with the vehicle's cylinder, careful not to gag or pull disgusted faces at having touched smelly metal. The girl would lose her already waning trust in me. Well, in Giridhar, but it would still be my doing. It was my task after all.

The girl looked on as I took out parts, and spent a few minutes cleaning them out, all the while using Giridhar's practised hands. After a couple of scratches on the man's palm, several opportunities to retch, and the pleasing sound of a running engine, I turned to the girl, casually wiping my hands on Giridhar's spotless handkerchief.

'There was a problem with the carburettor,' I explained, sounding knowledgeable about scooters and machines. 'See that sticky gum-like substance there? I've just cleaned it out. It was preventing the carburettor from working smoothly.' I wanted to say carburettor twice more; it made me sound so smart. The feeling of having much knowledge in any subject outside the domain of DC and Marvel was very alien to me.

The girl gaped at me with a mixture of wonder and gratitude. So this is what I looked like when Pranav fixed my laptop all those times, I thought.

'Thank you so much!' the girl squealed. 'So nice of you!'

'No problem,' I smiled.

The girl got on her vehicle and sped off into the traffic while I sat behind the car wheel, watching as an official tick mark appeared beside God's handwritten task. I smiled at the rear-view mirror as the gold in my aura increased by a fraction.

'Yay,' I grinned.

Like a giant waking from a deep slumber, the quietened soul inside Giridhar began to stir. Unwilling to spend precious minutes squabbling with it again, I swam out of the man's body. Crossing over to a Stop sign, I caught a glimpse of him blink in puzzlement at the grease stains on his handkerchief.

Chortling, I left Giridhar to his very confused thoughts and zoomed off to my next task.

❦

Disbelief imbued me as I stared at the Checklist.

You gotta steal from a homeless freak or I'll beat you with a white hot poker.

I was sitting in a deserted Cubbon Park. I was quite alone, save for the young couple seated on a park bench a few feet from the tree under which I sat. They'd spent a few minutes giggling and murmuring into each other's ears, but then the two had turned very quiet, which left very little to the imagination.

I consulted the Checklist again. The words had written

themselves in spiky black ink—Satan certainly had his own style.

I frowned as I tapped the scroll on my thigh. What could I possibly steal from someone who was so poor that they couldn't afford to put a roof above their head?

Steal from a homeless person—who did things like this? Well, Satan's minions, sure, but they'd been mortals before turning into imps, hadn't they? Did that mean people could get this bad?

I paused for a few moments and jogged down memory lane. I knew I'd done some bad things in my life, and I wasn't proud of them.

When I was eleven years old, a classmate's braid had become entangled with the zipper on my backpack. I knew full well that informing a teacher would help relieve Deepika's locks from the metal trap, but, always jealous of the class leader's grades, friends and pretty much everything, I'd grabbed a pair of scissors from the emergency sewing kit we were expected to carry, and chopped her hair free. I'll never forget the hatred in Deepika's teary brown eyes.

Another time, I was with Ria, a real chatter who could never shut up. The bimbo kept rubbishing my best friends. I couldn't take that, so I plonked my entire scoop of chocolate ice cream on her dress. I had finally discovered a way of rendering her speechless.

Most recently, I'd punctured the back tyre on my

neighbour's motorbike because he wouldn't stop stealing my newspaper. I'd told myself that it was okay; it didn't count as sin because he truly deserved it. I'd never once questioned the dubious morality of the act.

Until now. *Now* I knew why my aura had red in it. Sure, these were very juvenile acts, but they'd piled up little by little. I could've taken the high road on so many occasions but no, I'd taken the easy way out and been the absolute worst version of myself.

Red. Ugh. I hated the colour now. I hated the very idea of doing something wrong. I had no intention of stealing from a homeless person.

But, if I failed, what did Satan have in store for me? As they so often did in distressing circumstances such as these, awful thoughts took shape inside my head. Is Satan really going to burn me? Will he spray me with poison spittle? Will I spend eternity as an eerie wall hanging in his dark fortress? Damn it, will I have to start watching football and get on the Manchester United bandwagon?

Lost in thought, and torn between not wanting to complete the task and to avoid Satan's wrath (or worse, sarcasm), I failed to notice a dishevelled old man making his way past my tree. I turned when I heard the rustle of leaves as his feet dragged along, and his irritated mutterings, 'Why can't these people do their business somewhere else?'

The man was old, wrinkled, and covered in a ragged old

shirt. Maybe this was the old beggar V had spoken of. It had to be him. He was in Cubbon Park, too! I approached him slowly as he made his way to the shade of a banyan tree.

The wrinkled old man was muttering to himself.

'Who cares? No one cares for Nagaraj. I will die like this—poor, ragged, filthy.' He spat out a mouthful of paan. 'My son! Krishna! That rascal, that scoundrel! Killing people, looting their homes…he will be brought to justice one day, Nagaraj, just wait and see…he has brought you so much shame, so much hurt…something horrible will come upon that useless son of yours…'

I gazed at the man in pity. His hair was a matted knot. He wore thick glasses, eyes heavy with sadness. With his feet covered in cuts and bruises, it was a wonder he could even walk around. It almost broke me when he took off his threadbare shawl and placed it on the ground as a makeshift mattress.

Resting his head on his elbows, he drifted off into what must have been a very uneasy sleep, because his eyelids were still aflutter and he continued to mutter under his breath.

This man was in pain, I realized. It wasn't physical, though. It was worse. He was heartbroken.

I chewed my lip. I longed to ignore my task and help out this man. *Just go with your gut!* my inner voice screamed at me. Ignoring the smell of sweat and grime on the man's bare chest, I entered his body in one swift motion.

The sadness in the man's soul almost shattered me. Memories of bygone years when he used to be a husband and a father whooshed before my eyes. He had seen happy times before his house was snatched away by a rich builder. Soon, he'd been cast aside like useless scrap. His wife had died decades ago, succumbing to malaria. His son, a gangly seventeen year old then, had left home, spitting bitterly on the ground and calling his father a wastrel.

Newspapers bearing a picture of the son, a fully grown man now, swam in front of my eyes. He was on the run, wanted for killing an old couple and running away with their money.

The old man snored, and it was all I could do to stay put and get to work.

I summoned every ounce of mental power I had, and reached out to his soul. All that negativity, bitterness and sorrow, it was killing him from the inside—I could feel it draining me as well. Delicately, I engaged his soul, expelling negative thoughts from his memory for the time being, and polishing those of happier days he'd spent with his parents in his quiet village, of youthful years he'd lived laughing with friends in the tractor company, of unbounded joy he'd felt when he'd married the girl of his dreams. I soothed the bad memories and emboldened the happy ones.

Slowly, as I felt his soul grow less embittered, I prepared to let go. He was as thin as ever, but his face looked far more relaxed than before. I wanted to lend him a coat, a blanket, anything, but that was just wishful thinking.

The beggar's eyes flickered open and they immediately found the skies. I remembered a promise I'd made just this morning, and folded my hands to the heavens above.

Hey, V, Queen of Performers, if you're listening, and if you can really see your biggest fan from up there, he'd love to see you now.

Nothing happened.

Any gesture right about now will do!

V had come off as a performer who liked a bit more suppliance from her audience.

PLEASE, V! YOU'RE THE BEST! PLEASE!

I willed for something to happen, almost sweating from the effort of thinking positive thoughts.

It looked like V heard my plea because finally, something did come the old beggar's way.

A beautiful, multicoloured jacket descended from above, flapping its colourful sleeves, looking more like a tropical bird that an item of clothing. It fell gently on the man, wrapping him in an embrace that filled him with a very powerful feeling—cheer.

And then it hit me. Rainbows spread cheer, especially when people most needed it. Along with a bit of sunshine, they livened up a dull, gloomy day, just so that there could be a moment of cheer in an otherwise grey world. V was unique, after all, and it was a crime not to appreciate her.

I left the man's body only after thinking a very emphatic, *Thanks, V, that was brilliant!*

Well, you know what they say, said V's voice inside my head. *Where there's a will, there's a way, and a rainbow jacket.*

I grinned as I walked out of the park. But my joy was short-lived as soon as I glanced at the Checklist. I felt a sinking feeling in the vicinity of my stomach, because I knew I'd blown my first evil task. But, to my utter bewilderment, a spiky black tick mark appeared beside Satan's first assignment. Almost reluctantly, it seemed to me, my aura burned a little more gold.

And I understood. As I looked back at the homeless man, now covered blissfully in V's jacket, it dawned on me that I had, in fact, succeeded in stealing something from him—I'd robbed him of his pain.

5

Cakewalk

When the scroll presented me with my next task, I was still marvelling at how I'd managed to trick the Checklist into crossing out an evil task. The strange limitations of the Checklist kept me amused for a while, and I'd wandered around the city, hanging around at favourite haunts, a startling number of which just happened to sell cheese burgers. I was left in no doubt that I hadn't had the best dietary habits when I was alive.

It was now twilight in Bangalore. I was drifting over a weed-ridden lake, thinking wistfully about a hot meal and a soft bed. Not that I was hungry or tired. Food and mattresses, to a ghost, seemed neither a necessity nor a prerogative. I just missed these comforts I'd taken for granted.

I settled down on the branch of a tree by the lake, and in the fading light, looked at the golden words again.

Thou shalt bake a cake for someone you wronged.

My cousin's seventeenth birthday. That was the last time I had baked a cake. Even with my grandmother's expert guidance, the cake had been an unmitigated disaster. I didn't know how it had happened. One second, it had looked edible, and the next, it had acquired the consistency of congealed glue. I'd taken an oath that day: I would never subject anything with a sense of taste to my baking.

But now I was going to have to break that oath.

God didn't understand; I'd be wronging someone just by baking a cake for them.

What will I bake? Will it be Chocolate Catastrophe, Red-velvet Ruin or Treacle Tragedy? All for the reasonable price of one dead taste bud.

There was no alternative, no backdoor exit here. I simply had to make a pathetic excuse for dessert, and offer it to someone whom I will have then maltreated twice. Great.

I sighed and swung from the branch upside down like a bat. My world turned topsy-turvy!

I looked at the lights of Bangalore and let out a soft moan. I missed my city already. But I wondered—did it miss me?

My grandmother would leave the living room door open, and there'd be no one to remind her to shut it except the next-door neighbour, Meera aunty. Shirley would be in her room, nose-deep in the latest issue of *National Geographic*. Pranav and Rishi would be plotting the destruction of the world, or else summoning something else—the ghost of

Ravana, perhaps, with interesting mutations. Those two had maintained that having nine extra heads wasn't cool enough.

The terrace! I already missed my favourite spot in my block of apartments. The same terrace where I'd nearly fractured my leg playing football for the first (and last) time. My team had won four goals to two. I was told that that was good, but I hadn't honestly enjoyed playing a sport where ninety minutes of chasing a ball could actually end in a 0-0 score line.

A light breeze wafted in from the lakeside just as laziness draped its soothing arms around me. I still had a couple of days to go before I went back to the schizophrenic garden, I told myself. That left me with some time to spend on this tree. Procrastination, I decided, seemed like a fine idea.

The surrounding din of the city subsided, and I happily fell asleep, not noticing that I'd been wrong about ghosts and their rights to forty winks. And not noticing that my aura was turning a shade redder with every hour I had decided to waste.

'BAWWWWK!'

I would've jumped out of my skin if I'd had any.

A large brown bird was perched beside me, welcoming the new day with all the energy it had built up after a morning of worm-munching.

'And to think I found my bleeping alarm tone annoying,' I grumbled.

Groggy-eyed, and still irritated by my avian wake-up call, I abandoned my spot on the tree and looked up. The sun was already shining, but not so brightly as to render me blind. Clouds blanketed it ever so often, and I guessed it was maybe half past seven. I was thinking of getting some coffee before I realized I couldn't. The thought didn't cheer me up one bit.

'The afterlife is terrible!' I wailed at the winds, as if they would carry my message up to the clouds and everyone beyond.

When I'd been alive, mornings used to mean a cup of coffee, a plate of my grandmother's cooking, and her beautiful hundred-watt smile. All this followed by a brawl with the shameless newspaper-filching neighbour, of course. It had grown into a routine I'd come to enjoy over the years. OK, I said to myself. It's just a cake. Flour, sugar and some icing. You're a half-natural. You've got this. Just don't pull an Arundathi. And try to cork the screw-up bottle. I had to encourage myself. This was a do-or-die situation. Figuratively, of course.

Whom had I wronged recently? Well, there was Rishi, but I referred to him as an ape's bottom a dozen times a day. Meera aunty's face popped up next. I considered my neighbour for a full minute before striking her name off the Offended list. Somehow, pointing out that her going out for a walk clad in a nightie and towel didn't feel like a sin.

There had been an episode with Mithun, my milkman, a

few weeks ago. It had ended badly for the guy. My hand had accidentally made contact with his cheek when his fingers had accidentally brushed my butt and then groped it for good measure. What was I supposed to do, *not* leave an imprint of my hand on his face?

My brain practically wept through the next few minutes as I shuffled my memories like a pack of playing cards, desperate to find someone who'd help me complete my task.

Suddenly, a memory slithered out of its hidey-hole and began to play itself like an old movie. Shame prickled my neck.

It was time to apologize to Shalini.

I didn't like the girl, but given the way I'd dealt with what came to be known as the Runaway Sarong incident, I was ready to bet she wasn't my biggest fan either. That she would turn into one when she ate my cake was questionable, but I will have at least tried.

With my fingers balled into a fist of steely resolve, I soared off into the sky like a paper plane.

Eleven Candles was a large bakery in one of the quieter corners of Vijaynagar. Known for its peerless sprinkled doughnuts, it stood on a street overlooking a beautiful park. Rickety chairs were placed around scrubbed wooden tables outside the bakery, sheltered by large striped umbrellas, giving the whole place a nice, warm look.

It was my favourite place when I used to stay in Vijaynagar. That was a long time ago—six, maybe seven years. It was where I used to buy my birthday cakes from, meet my school friends, and fetch my grandmother some bread whenever she got sick. Also, I used to nick a potato bun or two, but I never chose to recall that particular memory.

All those times I was there, I never once asked the portly chef Mohan if I could take a quick peek at his kitchen. I'm sure he would've let me, I was his most loyal customer. Thieving customer, yes, but loyal just the same.

Now I didn't have to ask for permission to enter. Now I could just zoom into Mohan's kitchen through the keyhole on the closed door.

Which is exactly what I did.

I could've simply gone through the door, but this seemed more fun. It was a very odd sensation, squeezing in through the key-shaped crevice.

As I shrunk myself into it, I experienced something— I could feel parts of me blending in with the keyhole's metal body. I didn't have time to ponder over this, so I zipped out and emerged into the kitchen.

Oh, what a place! I instantly wanted to be a chef.

The baker's kitchen was spectacular. Tall shelves lined the walls, carrying rows and rows of flour, sugar, fruit and oil. The smell of freshly baked bread permeated the room. Cabinets were thrown open to reveal sets of identical bowls, spoons, plates and all kinds of moulds that I guessed were used for making cupcakes. Chopping boards were littered with small pieces of chopped up strawberries and oranges. The oven was turned on, and I could make out two trays laden with sponge-like things inside.

A narrow passage opened into a cooler inside in whose frozen compartments were arranged at least fifty bottles filled with different types of syrup—maple, raspberry, peppermint, orange, chocolate, almond, hazelnut, and so on—it was mind boggling. There was enough cream and butter inside the refrigerator to give at least five able gladiators a serious coronary.

Yes, I decided, if ever I were to be brought back to life by a crazy scientist, however gruesomely, I would become a pastry chef. It would be worth it just to spend eight hours a day crammed into a kitchen which smelled of toasted marshmallow all day long.

Mohan was busy at the large counter that separated the ovens from the shelves. I hovered at his elbow and watched in anticipation as his scrawny assistant brought him three eggs, a slab of butter, and a few other things in little packets.

'Ramesh,' Mohan sighed, his stubby hands on his hips, 'aren't you missing something?'

The assistant frowned at the table.

'Oh!'

'What "oh"? Such a basic thing, you stupid fellow!'

The assistant turned pink. 'I-I'll get it.'

'Just toss it here!'

I should've ducked at the word 'toss', but it didn't matter. The large ceramic bowl just soared through my head. What was the chef thinking, asking people to hurl heavy utensils across the room? Didn't he know how dangerous that was? Only the Scottish folk were allowed to do crazy things such as hurling heavy things across distances. Granted, the bowl was no tree trunk, but my point still stood.

My indignation went unnoticed, obviously, as Mohan began to create culinary magic.

It was like watching one of those master chef programmes in fast forward. Mohan's hands seemed to obey his brain's commands before they were fully formulated. Butter, eggs, sugar and buttermilk went into the bowl one after the other. Out of nowhere, a fancy whisk appeared in his palm and with some kind of sleight of hand, he beat the ingredients with a whirlpool motion. How on earth did he manage that without bedecking his surroundings with speckles of the butter and egg mix?

His was a soul I'd find impossible to beat. A man of such skill rarely played host to a weak spirit.

But it was half past eight already (had I spent thirty minutes gawping at the wonder that was baking powder?), and I had to get a move on if I meant to cross more tasks off the Checklist. It was time to brainstorm.

Should I Possess the assistant? Have him bake a cake? No, Mohan was clearly reluctant to let that boy anywhere near the counter. Having control over this boy was akin to having no control all.

The clock was ticking, the whisk was beating eggs and flour faster and faster still. The tiny, flexible, enchanted little whisk.

My lips widened in a sudden smile. The whisk!

I could Possess the utensils.

I'd be baking the cake in an indirect way. I could take hold of the whisk, the bowl, the oven, or whatever else suited my fancy. These objects were inanimate—this meant they had as much free will as the public of an authoritarian country. They'd be laughably simple to possess and command.

So that's what passing through the keyhole was about! I had actually almost Possessed it!

I bit my lower lip gleefully. It was soul manipulation time.

With my tongue sticking out through my lips, I plunged into the thin beams of the whisk. The steely surfaces were stiff, but the competition from their souls certainly wasn't. It took me about two seconds to settle into the whisk comfortably.

Banishing premature thoughts of victory from my mind, I turned my full attention to the bits of egg and blobs of butter, and pushed them around as Mohan willed. Amusement parks and their overpriced rides... hmmmmph, they couldn't hold a candle to the Whisk Whirl. I was enjoying myself so thoroughly that I'd almost forgotten why I was doing this. Almost.

Like unbidden rain clouds sauntering into the sky on a pleasant spring morning, nasty memories of the unfortunate Sarong incident wafted into my brain as my wet cake mixture slowly smoothened.

Semester break. Five months ago. Rishi, Pranav, Shirley and I were holidaying on the sandy beaches of Malpe in Udupi. It was a balmy evening and the rest of our friends from college were still near the cottages, so we had the beach to ourselves. Gentle waves crashed the shores, slapping our feet as we laughed hysterically at Rishi's latest obsession.

I whisked a little harder, ordering my mind to focus.

'A ghost? Seriously, Rishi?' Shirley shrieked in mirth even as Rishi asserted he had seen one near his portico, stooping low to pick up a fallen rose. 'Even ghosts stop to smell roses, then?' I'd punched him on the arm as I smirked.

Vanilla extract descended on the whisk's handle as Mohan added it to the bowl.

The sky turned scarlet as the sun sunk into the watery depths of the sea. We clambered onto our scooters and drove off into the town. Shirley sat behind Pranav, and Rishi behind me. We passed a large group of friends by a small coffee stall—Shalini, Dhruv and Rohan. We stopped to chat with the three, much to my displeasure, because I never could stand Shalini. Wild turkeys were smarter than her.

I traversed the bowl without losing my resolve to help bake a masterpiece. I didn't want to be reminded of the events that followed.

'Nice sarong, Shalini,' Rishi said with a foolish smile. I wanted to smack him, the idiot. 'Thank you,' Shalini crooned. She stepped closer to us and tousled Rishi's hair. The amount of bling around her neck could've cause a countrywide seizure. 'I like your T-shirt. It's fab. Totally awesome, yo!' Rishi looked about ready to turn into a puddle of schmaltzy goo. I was about ready to retch.

The smell of mingled butter and vanilla was scintillating as I threw myself into the beams, sending fresh bursts of energy pumping through the whisk.

'I'll see you guys around, maybe get a drink later?' winked Shalini as I revved up the scooter's engine. 'Yeah, that'd be fab!' I said over-enthusiastically. I felt Rishi poke me on the back of my head reproachfully.

'Did you pre-heat the oven, Ramesh?' Mohan said.

Out of the corner of my beams' eye, I caught sight of Ramesh's bobbing head. I supposed the eggs would soon be beaten enough. I wanted to give the final round of whipping my all. I was sorry for the way I'd behaved. I was sorry I had wronged Shalini the way I had. I wished I could take it back, but I couldn't.

Shalini hugged all of us as if leaving our company for good. Or so I secretly hoped—I'd always been a little jealous of the girl. I felt her sarong brush my leg. I frowned slightly, wondering if the flimsy material might snag itself in the Activa's several protrusions. But I couldn't care less. A part of me wanted to leave her red-faced. I rode off. A split second later, a scream echoed across the empty streets, and Pranav and I brought our scooters to an immediate halt, alarmed. There was Shalini, a few paces behind us, desperately shielding her bare legs with her hands, to no avail; her sarong had wrapped itself around my side-stand.

Anger boiled at the pit of my stomach, urging me to whip faster and faster. I should've felt nothing but sympathy for Shalini. I should've been more comforting. I should've done anything other than what I'd done.

Rishi leapt off the vehicle. He broke into a run, taking with him as much of the sarong he could disentangle. When the flimsy skirt-like piece couldn't cover Shalini, he pulled off his jacket at once and helped her drape it around her hips. Shirley was saying something in a soothing voice and Pranav was doing an excellent job of staring at his toes. I blinked twice and turned away, not wanting to face Shalini. I could see her disbelieving, angry face in my rear-view mirror as I rode off as fast as I could, half a sarong still around my stand.

Mohan stopped churning, and carelessly dropped the whisk I was occupying into a plastic mug filled with water. The final traces of liquid butter dripped into the mug, turning the water a sludgy yellow. I slowly left the tool, passed through the mug, and without pausing to think, took my place in the small bowl which the chef was talking about using for the cocoa.

As he stirred unsweetened cocoa powder, salt and flour, I thought about what had happened. I'd made a mistake by not apologizing. Sure, it hadn't been my fault, not entirely. But the minute I'd sensed her sarong might get entangled, I should've said something, I should've had the compassion to turn around and ease her discomfort after the embarrassing mishap. I hadn't. I'd turned away like a coward; a heartless girl with skin as thick as a rhino's. I'd deserved Shalini's cold shoulder ever since that day. It was no wonder that she'd shunned not only me, but my friends as well. And that included Rishi.

Rishi, the simpering buffoon who'd lent her his jacket when she'd most needed it. Rishi, the romantic fool who'd been hopelessly in love with her since the day he'd held her hair back in that nightclub as she threw up into a dustbin. Those were moments of burning passion which Rishi chose to throw in my face whenever I teased him about falling for such a bimbo.

'We should put it in for how many minutes, Ramesh?' Mohan quizzed his assistant.

After the most disappointing pause that could trail a teacher's question, Ramesh chirped. 'Thirty.'

'Sure?'

'Yes, yes,' replied the assistant, wiping a bead of sweat off his brow.

'Put the pan in, then.'

I had a moment's break between leaving a brand new spatula, and inhabiting the oven. Dreading the prospect of abandoning the sweet-smelling, cocoa-covered spatula and entering an object with ten times a desert's temperature, I spread out thin and glued myself to the inner surfaces of the oven.

Hot. Hot. Hot. I was literally in a furnace. Even as a ghost, I could feel the heat.

The oven's soul was very understanding, though. It offered to lower its temperature every few minutes so that I'd get a breather, but I declined this generosity, explaining that if it malfunctioned, it would most likely be returned to the factory and promptly turned into metal mulch. The offer was withdrawn almost immediately.

The cake puffed as the timer counted down. My eyes took in its rise, all spongy and delicious. It was a marvel to behold, and it was a marvel I'd helped make. Trickling through all that anger and guilt I was feeling, came a thin stream of pride that calmed my senses a little.

The oven timer sounded loudly, and my ears throbbed in protest. I rushed out of it and took refuge atop a shelf before I could die again.

'Sir, sir, sir!' Ramesh's excited yells annoyed me more than the blaring timer.

'Ramesh, Ramesh, Ramesh!' Mohan yelled back, as he

pulled on a pair of revolting green mittens and extracted the cake carefully. 'Yeah! Annoying isn't it?'

Ramesh looked like he was bursting with any number of unintelligent retorts, but held them back.

'Is the cake ready, sir?'

'No, I love poking toothpicks into mounds of chocolatey sponge just for fun,' replied Mohan.

Satan would've been proud of the man's sarcasm. Mohan took off his mittens and wagged a threatening finger at his assistant.

'Now, this cake might well be the best one I've made yet.' I let out a sigh of relief. 'Let it cool for five minutes. Don't rush the frosting.' He paused. 'Shalini madam will have your head if you mess up her cake.'

I slipped off the shelf. Coincidences were fun to hi-five on, but this particular one simply took me by shock. Mohan went on.

'It's her friend's birthday today, and she wants the icing to be in blue. Name is spelt D-H-R-U-V. She'll be in at noon, so, ready it by then. I'm going home; it's my wedding anniversary, for heaven's sake. I want to make something for my wife for a change.'

And with that, he threw off his apron, huffed out of the kitchen, and drove away in his car.

I looked at the cake with a startled smile on my face. Mohan had said it could be the best cake he might've baked yet. Maybe a sincere apology did work miracles sometimes, I thought, as the reassuring tick mark appeared on the Checklist.

6

A Bonus Task

Shalini swung by at lunchtime, clutching a handbag big enough to carry four other handbags and a Great Dane. In her glittering heels and with her straightened hair, she looked like a repurposed Barbie with a serious hair-clip addiction.

She approached the doughnut counter and rapped her knuckles on it, narrowly missing my knees.

'Hello? Boss!'

Ramesh came rushing out of the store room, wiping his palms on his apron.

'What, what, I didn't spill the—oh, Shalini madam! Come, come, your cake is ready.'

'I wanna see it before I pay,' Shalini said with unnecessary aggression.

The assistant nodded vigorously and disappeared into the store room. He emerged again, with his diminutive torso hidden behind a large cardboard box.

'Show me, show me, show me,' Shalini squealed.

I hovered next to Ramesh as he lowered the box onto the counter and let Shalini examine the cake. She chewed her lower lip with a look that suggested there was something nasty under her nose.

'The icing…'

Ramesh adopted a concerned look.

'Y-you ordered blue, we did blue only, madam.'

'I wanted a bluer blue. This is too… like, aqua, know what I mean?'

I shared Ramesh's bemused expression. What did it matter how blue the icing was when its entire life cycle involved a short trip from the top of the cake to Dhruv's cheeks?

'But, madam…' Ramesh began uncertainly.

Shalini clicked her tongue. 'Whatever, no time now. How much for this?'

As she paid the owner of Eleven Candles, balancing the box in one hand, I grew worried that she would let the box fall to the floor—I had long suspected that her sense of balance was likely to be way off due to her big head. But Shalini managed to strut across the bakery floor and out into the bustling street with the spongy cake with its not-as-blue-as-blue icing perfectly intact. In the suffusion of heavy perfume and arrogance she left behind, I breathed a sigh of relief. So far, so good.

Stepping out of the bakery, I thrust a hand into my back

pocket and extracted the Checklist to see what Satan expected of me next.

Cause an accident. I mean it, numbskull. I'm talking about roads paved with jam here.

The urge to throw up all over the Checklist was overwhelming.

Satan had the savoir faire of a drooling Rottweiler. Roads paved with jam? Cannonballs have been kinder, I thought with a numb feeling spreading from my fingertips to my head.

I shoved the scroll into my pocket and looked around hopelessly. Things had gone really well until now: the punctured tyre, the homeless man and the cake. I should've known it was too good to last.

A cyclist was making his way past the bakery, whistling merrily to himself. An auto crossed the road, coming dangerously close to the cyclist, but they didn't collide. If Satan had forced a hand, if I weren't so conflicted about good and evil, I would've already turned the poor men into a gory heap of human bones and sinew.

But I couldn't. The impish beast inside me didn't stir. In all eternity, I would not be able to effect the loss of innocent lives.

The tall clock tower in the corner of the street chimed, and I started convulsively. It was one o'clock in the afternoon. My hours were numbered (again), and I had no idea how to take the next step without the prospect of eternal guilt and shame.

Or maybe you won't have to feel guilty, whispered a voice inside me. *Maybe you're meant to do this.*

Stop, I said to the voice, half-heartedly.

Arundathi, you know yourself better than anyone. You know you can do this, the voice hissed.

But this is so wrong! I countered.

Wrong. Right. It's such a blurred line right now, isn't it? What if someone crossed you? You would wield your axe, would you not? Would that be wrong?

I... but... shut up!

The voice kept whispering, egging me on, and urging me to go through with my task. Feeling a little faint, I made to sit down on the pavement.

'OI!' came a voice from behind.

I jumped so violently that the wind hoisted me all the way up to the top of a tree. From my awkward perch atop it, I looked down at the pavement. Where there been no one a moment before, sat a young boy of around fourteen years.

He was looking up at me through the fluttering leaves. On his head he wore a bright red cap which hid most of his neon green hair. His T-shirt was splashed with the colours of a sports team whose name I couldn't pronounce without sounding like a crow with a sore throat, and his jeans looked like they hadn't seen a washing machine since the dinosaurs had last walked the planet.

He looked like someone with a sprightly countenance, but

he appeared to be, at the moment, distraught. Overwhelming instinct told me that this boy would do me no harm.

I slid down the tree trunk and approached him.

'Are you alright?'

He looked at me with warm brown. Those mischievous eyes and that springy hair buzzed with familiarity.

'I didn't see you here,' I said, sitting down beside him.

'Sorry,' the boy mumbled. 'I have that kind of appearance. Tend to melt into the background.'

I eyed his vivid green hair but said nothing of it.

'You scared the daylights out of me, kiddo.'

'Funny,' frowned the boy. 'And I thought *you* were the ghost in this equation.'

I flashed him a grin which faltered within a second.

'Wait. You can see me! How?' My fingers immediately darted to my pocket. I felt relieved—the Middler's necklace was still there. I hadn't activated my visibility booster.

'Hey, you have your powers, I have mine,' the boy shrugged.

I raised an eyebrow.

'Oh? And what do you know of my powers?'

He nodded at the bakery.

'That was some brilliant Possession down there. I wouldn't have thought a whisk could be so neatly controlled. Nice.'

I felt a stone drop into my stomach.

'Are you ... stalking me?' I could hear the panic in my

voice. 'Are you an Imp? Has…the Dolce man sent you to sway me? Speak up!'

But the boy's eyes mirrored only confusion.

'Dolce who?' Before I could answer, the boy waved a hand. 'Actually, don't explain. You'll probably go into a rant. Ghosts are always so angry, or mopey, like their life is over.' He caught my stare. 'Oh, sorry. But you know what I mean!'

'Mmm,' I grunted. The boy went back to staring at the gravel lining the side of the street.

Through the corner of my eye, I observed him. He had a thin, wiry frame which seemed to be diminishing with every passing second. He looked so miserable and burdened with some unknown weight, it seemed to outweigh the enormity of my own present predicament.

'Bee in your bonnet?' I asked gently.

The boy sighed. Somehow, that small act made him look much older than his years.

'Giant bee with a nasty sting, yeah.' He crossed his legs. 'I have this assignment, and I have no idea how I'm going to finish it.'

Kids these days, I thought. They couldn't get through a piece of homework without going into clinical depression.

'Lay it on me. What's the subject?'

The boy kicked a stone across the street where it hit a bicycle tyre and rolled off.

'Really want to know what's up with me? Trust me, you

won't believe half of it.'

'Shoot,' I said, miming as though I were eating from an invisible bucket of popcorn.

The boy scratched the back of his neck hesitantly, and then launched into his tale of woe.

'A month ago, I was sent out on an assignment. Field work, you see. It's called TSOC—Two Subjects One Collaboration. Bring two subjects together to form one super subject, kind of like combining English Literature and English Grammar. I was given every minute detail about both the subjects—lists, detailed descriptions, everything. I had one job to do: complete the collaboration without altering either subject's details. With me so far?' he asked me.

'It's not exactly quantum physics. Just continue,' I said.

'Exactly,' said the boy weepily. 'It's not quantum physics. So, I should've managed it with ease, right? Wrong. I botched it up. The subjects' lists were upset, and I failed my assignment. So, to set things right, I requested...'

'Extra credits?' I interjected.

'Yeah, I guess you could call it that,' replied the boy thoughtfully. 'A week ago, I was sent on another TSOC assignment. But this time, no lists, no descriptions. I'm all on my own. I set out brimming with self-confidence despite my previous faux pas, believing in myself that I will finish the assignment and all that. But now, I'm in a pickle. I managed to study one subject, but that was six days ago. I was supposed to have linked it to the other one by now.' He paused to chew his fingernails. 'The deadline is midnight, which leaves me with eleven hours before I'm busted. I don't think I can finish this. I haven't found the other subject.'

Thin creases lined my forehead.

'Right, when you say you haven't *found* the subject, do you mean a textbook or some notes?'

'Nooo!' whined the boy. 'I cannot find the subject, don't you understand? The subject is missing!'

Thoughts raced through my head. Either this boy was really bad at basic grammar, mixing up his verbs like a toddler. Or he was speaking in code. But his spoken English seemed flawless, so I supposed he was in some sort of secret club which had sent him out on a stupid dare.

The creases on my forehead deepened. It was time to glean some clarity on this matter.

'Is this schoolwork?'

'Well,' said the boy slowly. 'It's definitely not homework.'

Shrewd, I thought.

'Hmmm,' I offered, pausing to think for a minute. Then, 'So, this subject—what is it? History? Economics?'

But the boy wasn't listening. He was staring curiously at me.

'Hey,' he said brightly. '*You* could help me out with this ...'

'Er, not if it's Physics, I almost failed that subject. All that balancing equation stuff was maddening.'

'That's Chemistry.'

'See what I mean?'

The boy breathed in deeply and looked at me with large, beseeching eyes.

'If I explained in greater detail, would you help me?'

'Sure.'

'Okay, first things first. Hi, my name is Sarandip, but you can called me Saran.' He managed a small smile.

'Arundathi,' I said.

'Nice name.'

'Thanks.' I rose from the pavement. 'So, your assignment?'

'It's actually straightforward,' Saran said. We began to move down the road. 'The two subjects? They're people. I merely adopted the technical term, shall we say. One's a girl, the other's a boy.'

I groaned. 'Please tell me you're not trying to hitch the two.'

Saran gave me an apologetic grin. 'Yeah, I'm a walking dating-slash-matrimonial site.'

'Who in their right minds gives such assignments to adolescents?' I threw my hands up in the air.

'It's a social experiment sort of thing,' said Saran.

I rolled my eyes. The things schools made children do these days was enough to send the brightest minds on a shopping spree for self-administrable straitjackets.

'Fine, so you have to play Cupid now?' I asked.

Saran's lips twitched at mention of Cupid. 'I have to adopt a more indirect approach.'

'Like what—romance and courtship? As if this romance stuff even works,' I scoffed.

'Sure it does,' Saran bobbed his head. 'My father believes in it.'

'Yeah, well, he's deluded.' I hated that I sounded so bitter.

'Something tells me your love life has been simply thriving so far.'

I had to admire his ability to be snarky in the light of his unsolved problems.

'So, what's his name?' he asked hesitantly.

'None of your business,' I snapped.

'Come on,' he cajoled. 'It's just a name. It's not like I'll turn you two into my subjects. It wouldn't work even if I did—he's not going to be able to see you now anyway,' he added cheekily.

'Nikhil,' I said after a long pause. 'His name is Nikhil.'

'I see,' was all Saran said.

I sensed it was time to change the topic. 'Tell me more about these subjects of yours.'

'Alright,' said Saran, hands fiddling with cap. 'Well, the girl's nice. Good-looking, charming, and very popular at her college, by the looks of it. She reads, had her nose in one book the whole of last night. She can write a thesis on vampires, I think. She's nineteen years old. Very cute. In fact, I can show you.'

He pulled out a phone from his jeans. The whole thing was by held together a lot of tape. He jabbed a bunch of buttons and showed me a photo of a group of girls in their late teens.

'See the one in the yellow T-shirt? That's her.'

I took a close look at the girl. She was pretty—oval face, shiny hair and petite.

'Whoa!' I gasped.

Saran yanked the phone away in alarm.

'What's the matter with you?'

'That girl... I know her! I've seen her somewhere,' I said quickly. I racked my brain. Where had I seen her before? And then, with the clarity of a DSLR camera, I remembered.

'I fixed her scooter yesterday! Near Silk Board! That's the girl! Wow!' I did a funny little jig.

'Calm down!' said Saran, tugging at my arm. I stopped waving my arms like a giant bird. Wiping the phone screen with the end of his T-shirt, he found another photo. 'It's splendid that you know one teenager. Hearty congratulations. Now see this guy I have to set her up with.'

I leaned forward, still smiling broadly.

He was tall and broad-shouldered, with a strong jaw. An easy smile stretched across his face, all the way up to his friendly eyes which seemed to brighten up the screen. He had an arm around a friend, who was looking at him with an amused expression, as if he'd said something extremely funny.

The very sight of him should've made me break into that happy jig. Instead, my smile peeled off my face like old paint off a ceiling. I blanched, even more than I had just by becoming a ghost.

Saran looked at me with concern.

'What's wrong? Something about this guy? Do you know him?'

I felt numb.

'Yeah,' I said quietly. 'That's Nikhil.'

I was seven years old when I first met Nikhil. I had commemorated our first play date by pouring a glass of banana milkshake on his head. Nikhil had responded in kind, resulting in a physical fight between the two of us. I went home with a broken nail, Nikhil went home with a broken tooth. My grandmother had administered a sound beating soon afterwards, and I'd gone to Nikhil's house with a huge slab of chocolate and a handwritten note of apology.

After an official ceasefire had been negotiated by the elders, we became thick friends (the power of chocolate never ceased to amaze me) and remained close even after I'd moved to a different neighbourhood at the age of sixteen. Although we didn't see each other, we'd kept in touch through phone and email. But I'd seen Nikhil a year ago at a mutual friend's engagement party. One look at him in that blue kurta and I'd fallen head over heels in love, that too with a boy I'd once decorated with a banana beverage, mind you.

Never having felt anything quite this strong for anyone else before, I was consumed by nervousness, and never once told him how I felt. It was stupid, silly and juvenile. The only things I knew about present day Nikhil was that he loved playing squash and visiting Blossom Book House. That's all. All my feelings had sprung from the way he'd looked in blue. They weren't true—that's what I told myself every time I thought about him.

But it had been eight months since that engagement party, and I hadn't looked at anyone else. It had helped that my college was filled with boys who were really just mammoths with the cranial capacity of an earthworm.

Nikhil had no idea how I'd felt about him. And now there was no way of telling him. But that didn't mean that I was prepared to let go, and spring to the aid of a teenager whose assignment would send Nikhil into the slender arms of an atrociously cute girl. Whose hair looked that good, anyway? Life was unfair, and the afterlife was even more so.

'Hello? Saran to Arundathi, Saran to Arundathi.'

I blinked out of my reverie, and my surroundings came into sharper focus. Saran and I were standing on Church Street. I hadn't realized how fast we'd got here. Maybe over-thinking the rules of afterlife romance shortened one's travel time.

'Your eyes look glazed. Do you have a concussion?' said Saran peering into my face like a doctor, and tapping my forehead with his knuckles.

'I don't,' I snapped. 'And stop practising Morse code on my forehead!'

Saran backed away from me. 'Hey, don't get all shirty with me. I'm not responsible for not telling Nikhil about your feelings, you dig?'

I wanted to dig a hole and jump into it. Instead, I found myself forcing further conversation.

'Why are we standing at the entrance to Blossom's?' I shot at Saran.

'You were mumbling as you walked,' Saran shrugged. 'Something something banana milkshake, blah blah blah kurta. And that Nikhil likes to spend his time at Blossom Book House.'

I felt a sheepish expression wash over my face. 'Didn't realize I was saying that stuff out loud.'

'It was funny,' Saran chortled.

'Yeah, I'm sure it was,' I muttered, glancing at the entrance to the bookstore. 'I don't know if he'll be here. It's the middle of the day, and the store looks sort of deserted.'

Saran gave me a strange look.

'You could be right. There's a very good chance he isn't in there. In which case, we'd be wasting precious minutes. He'd slip out of our grasp, and maybe end up miserable and alone for the rest of his life. Or,' he paused and looked me square in the eye, 'he *could* be in there, and we could make him meet someone who could make him very, very happy. Then again, it's up to you. I don't want to force you into anything that makes you uncomfortable, even if it ends up helping you, well, move on.'

I stared at Saran in astonishment. The last teenager I'd heard make so much sense was non-existent. There was too much truth in this boy's words to deny it.

I sighed. Maybe Nikhil would be inside Blossom's. Maybe we'd find him and bring him to Scooty girl's path. Maybe their fates would collide. Saran was right, there was no way we could be together now that he couldn't even see me. I had no idea what Nikhil liked in girls, but I was prepared to wager 'ghost-like personality' wouldn't make the cut. Nobody wanted a literal 'soul' mate, after all.

'Let's do it,' I nodded with grim determination.

'Excellent,' chirped Saran. 'So, we just go inside? No entrance fee or anything?'

I chuckled, in spite of myself.

'Entrance fee? What is this, a fair? Just follow me, kiddo, I know exactly where he might be in this store. If I remember our last conversation correctly, he's got his nose buried in the Thriller section.'

7

Tales in Red

'I want only *that* book, Mummy!' cried the little kid in khaki shorts, tugging at his mother's dupatta.

'Keep your voice down, Abhi!' snapped the tall woman as she continued to peruse the book her child was demanding.

The kid screwed his eyes shut and wailed loudly, but no tears rolled down his cheeks.

'I want it, mummy. I want it,' he pleaded, swinging off his mother's arm now.

The woman shook herself free of his grip. 'Stop making so much noise, Abhi. Go find Nikhil. We'll leave soon, go on.'

Saran and I were on the first floor of Blossom's, leaning against the comic book shelves. The air smelled of old books in which most people claimed to find magic. The only thing I'd ever really found in that smell was an overpowering nausea.

Saran gave me an excited look.

'Hear that? Lover boy is here!'

I nodded listlessly and watched Nikhil's younger brother wipe his perfectly dry cheeks and bolt from the Children's section. Without looking, he turned sharply round the corner and—

'OW!' he bumped into a pillar of flesh and bones wearing a pair of jeans and brown sandals.

'Are you okay?' I heard the girl turn and ask.

I drifted forward with Saran in tow, and together, we looked at the girl. So did Abhi, pushing himself to his feet and rubbing his knees. 'Yes, yes, I'm okay,' he mumbled, blushing embarrassedly. 'Sorry, bye!' And he ran off again, calling out for his brother.

The kid was cute. Then again, he was Nikhil's brother. Good hair and bright eyes ran in the family, I supposed.

'I'm going to check for Nikhil on the third floor,' said Saran.

I nodded absently, and continued to watch the girl as she turned her attention back to the books arranged haphazardly on the shelves. I glided along the aisle. She seemed to be a fan of crime thrillers. Half her book basket was already full of Lee Childs.

The shelves were stacked with hundreds of books but not the one she was hunting for, evidently. Standing on the balls of her feet, she craned her neck to get a better look at the dusty top rows. I caught sight of several books I would never touch even if I were alive.

The girl clicked her tongue in obvious disappointment, and stepped back from the shelves. Her gaze dropped to the lower rows, and after a good rummaging, her face filled with glee at the sight of a book bound in black leather.

She squatted and mouthed, '*Tales of Red* by William—'

'Goldberg, yes!' an ecstatic voice behind her exclaimed.

The girl and I both jumped up at the voice.

It was Nikhil. Dressed in a simple white T-shirt and blue jeans, he looked perfect.

Before the girl could register what was happening, he stooped, pulled *Tales of Red* out of the shelf and dropped it into his plastic basket. Without a word, he swept past the girl and ambled to the far end of the aisle.

She blinked furiously. I was surprised too. What had just happened? I thought.

But looking at the girl and Nikhil, something clicked in my mind. I had a strong feeling this girl was better suited for Nikhil than the subject Saran had studied. For one, she wasn't staying up reading vampire fiction. I wanted to Possess her to urge her forward and talk to Nikhil.

But before I could proceed with my plan, adjusting her glasses, the girl walked up to Nikhil, her basket swinging at her side.

'Excuse me?'

Nikhil looked over his shoulder with his eyebrows raised. 'Yeah?'

'Um,' she said in a small voice. 'That book you've got—*Tales of Red*—I, er, do you think—see, I've been looking for that one for—maybe, I don't know, could you...?'

A playful grin was starting to play along the sides of Nikhil's lips. I forced back a simpering smile. Now wasn't the time to turn into a giddy, love-struck twelve-year-old.

'You want the book,' he said.

The girl nodded.

'Maybe you should've picked it up instead of admiring the cover?' said Nikhil teasingly.

The girl looked a tad annoyed.

'I wasn't...' she bristled, and then appeared to change her mind. 'OK, never mind. Keep it.'

With that, she turned away, her ears turning red.

What? I thought, wanting to shake this girl. You're just going to give up? He took the book you've been hunting for for ages! Go get it, for heaven's sake!

Her back was to me as she once again stood at the Thriller section, her spectacled eyes randomly checking out the book titles in front of her. She was quite obviously fuming.

Just then, her phone rang, and she yanked it out. 'Hello!' she barked into it. 'Yes, what is it, Ma? No, I'm at Blossom's now. I got the bread and jam at Nilgiris half an hour ago!' She rolled her eyes. 'I'll be back soon. No, I didn't find that book.' She shot Nikhil a nasty sidelong look. 'Yes, bye.'

She dropped the phone into her bag and prepared to

leave the bookstore, much to my annoyance. I had to do something, anything, before they went their separate ways and never saw each other again. Before I could even conceive a plan, Saran came bounding down the staircase, and into the Thriller section.

'Hey, no luck upstairs, did you find...'

I drove my fist into his gut to make him shut up. Nikhil was approaching the girl.

Saran gave me a reproachful look. 'What are you doi...?' He followed my gaze. 'Whoa, isn't that—wait, what's he doing, talking to Geek of the Year?'

'If you could shut up for a second, maybe we would know more,' I said through gritted teeth.

Saran mimed zipping his lips together. We edged closer to Nikhil, who was now a few feet from the girl.

'Hey,' Nikhil said.

The girl spun around.

'I have an idea,' said Nikhil.

The girl (and I) raised our eyebrows. 'Yes?'

'We both want the book,' stated Nikhil.

'Right.'

'But, I have it with me.'

'Wow, world's shortest story ever,' muttered the girl.

Nikhil laughed airily. 'Care to add a paragraph or two to it?' he asked.

The girl chewed her lips.

Nikhil took a deep breath and said, 'How about you take the book...'

'Yes!' she said immediately.

'I'm not done,' he grinned. 'You take the book, on one condition.'

'And what's that?'

Nikhil hesitated. He looked nervous.

'You give it back to me...when we meet for lunch next Saturday.'

The girl looked taken aback, albeit pleasantly. I knew how she felt. I'd seen them all; the kind that slipped you a paper napkin at a Coffee Day outlet with a phone number scribbled across it, complete with a creepy smiley and everything; the kind that whistled at you at lonely street corners; the kind that chatted you up inside a bus even if you had earphones on. Their efforts constantly redefined a lack of imagination. But Nikhil was smooth. Four years inside various bookstores, and this hadn't once happened to me. To my surprise, I found the girl nodding to Nikhil's proposition.

'Alright, I'll lend you the book next week...'

'Great,' he smiled.

'I'm not done yet,' she said, copying him. 'I have one condition too.'

'Oh?' Nikhil swung his basket back and forth.

'I pick the spot where we meet—either the basketball court opposite Malleshwaram Association, or the Hockey

Grounds near Garuda Mall. Meet me at one of those places at one o'clock next Saturday, and if we happen to be at the same place at the same time, the book's all yours. Is that an acceptable deal?'

'No.' Nikhil smiled. 'It's an acceptable *date*.'

He dropped the book into the girl's basket and walked away. Saran and I gaped at each other.

'He's got the Devil's charm,' Saran said, sounding awed. 'Wish he'd save some for my first subject.'

'Hold on,' I said sharply to Saran. 'We are not setting him up with that Doll Face, no way. This girl seems way more real, and more Nikhil's type than the Vampire!'

'That wasn't our agreement!' cried Saran.

'Nikhil deserves a nice, sensible girl who can match him and challenge him. He doesn't need an idiot who finds depth in disturbing teen fetishes,' I argued. 'Either I help you bring geeky girl and Nikhil together, or I go my own way right now, and you'll be left to fend for yourself,' I added coolly.

Saran mouthed angrily at me. I didn't budge. For a few minutes, he huffed as he watched the girl get her books billed and leave the bookstore.

'Fine!' he caved. 'Six days of hard work down the drain, but I'll attach Nikhil to this nerd.'

I pulled a disgusted face. 'Could you not say "attach"? It sounds as if you're performing a ghastly surgery.'

'Surgeries are easier, believe me,' Saran mumbled.

We exited Blossom's. I stopped in the middle of the road, just because I could afford to.

'So, they're meeting next Saturday at Malleswaram or Garuda Mall,' I said to Saran.

'I can't wait until next Saturday!' Saran shook his head. 'My deadline's tonight, remember?'

I threw my hands up hopelessly. 'What are we supposed to do then?'

Saran scratched his head. A light bulb seemed to flash in his head all of a sudden and he snapped his fingers.

'Go get her back here, I'll take care of the rest.'

'Huh?'

'Just bring her here,' Saran said urgently, already walking away from me.

'To the entrance of Blossom's?' I shouted as a motorcycle passed through me.

Saran stopped in his tracks just to throw me an incredulous look. 'No, to the middle of the bloody street! *Yes,* to the entrance, duffer, now go!'

Slightly annoyed at being reprimanded by a teenage boy, I flew past a dingy hookah joint and cast my eyes around Church Street for the girl. Jeans and sandals... Where had she disappeared?

She was turning the corner when my eyes finally fell on her. It was time to commence Operation Take Control of Geek Girl.

❦

I needed just ninety seconds to hush this girl's soul. She was still reeling from setting an almost-date with a cute guy at a bookstore. Part of me wanted to banish all images of Nikhil from her memory, part of me wished she would cling to them even harder.

As I Possessed her, I learnt a lot about her. The girl's name was Vandana. She was a student of architecture, and her brain was buzzing with at least two thousand ideas per second. I was impressed, as my mind was only ever accustomed to the gibber-gabber of characters on TV, and a few dozen comic books. If intelligence was a measure of how much knowledge one possessed about the Incredible Hulk and Sandman, I'd be at par with Einstein.

Vandana's soul gave in to my persuasion so abruptly, I wished it hadn't been so—suddenly, I turned around on instinct. Sure enough I could hear the screeching sounds of the approaching vehicle. I almost got her hit by a BMW, whose driver halted the car before it could hit the girl.

'Watch where you're going, aunty!' he yelled before swerving around us and speeding off again.

Slightly abashed at being called an aunty, Vandana's soul made to retaliate before I silenced it again. I couldn't believe I was advocating tolerance. Wow, how the irascible have fallen, I thought.

Out of the corner of Vandana's eye, I could see Saran talking to a boy and a woman who appeared to be his mother—Nikhil and his mom. There was no time to waste. Saran was already dragging the family back to the bookstore. I jogged back to Blossom's, feeling the wind pick up Vandana's hair and toss it around her face. As Blossom's grew nearer, I slowed to a walk, but Saran mouthed from a few feet away.

'*RUN!*'

I broke into a run. The boy had a plan, after all (I hoped). Saran was a few feet ... inches away from me now. I was surely going to crash into the kid. But in the nick of time, Saran stepped out of the way. I wasn't quite as quick.

WHAM!

I rammed into Nikhil with so much force, I was jerked out of Vandana's form and sent flying across the narrow lane. I watched helplessly as the flap on her bag flew open, sending its contents crashing down onto the road. A purse, a half-eaten packet of Lays, and a can of pepper spray littered the ground around Nikhil's feet. Vandana's arms hugged thin air as a loaf of bread rolled out after the pepper spray. There was a tinkle of breaking glass as a jar smashed, painting the road with sticky red jam. The copy of *Tales of Red* fell on top of the jam, its pages instantly staining.

Nikhil turned to Vandana with a wide grin spreading across his face.

'We seem destined to meet again.'

'I don't know why I came back,' Vandana snapped, lifting the book off the road.

'I think it's fate,' Nikhil quipped.

'Yeah, right,' Saran snorted beside me. 'Like that idiot Fate could ever design this.'

I gave him a quizzical look, but he quelled it with a dismissive wave of his hand.

A smirk had worked its way into Nikhil's words. 'How fitting that the book is called *Tales in Red*. I like my books jam-stained.' He gave Vandana an incredulous look. 'Who puts a book alongside *jam*?'

Vandana clicked her tongue.

'I didn't know the bottle would break! Or that I would—'

'—crash into me like a bulldozer.'

Silence fell as the two of them stared at the book, the jam, and finally at each other.

'I'm Nikhil.' He offered her a hand to shake.

Take it, you fool, I willed silently. Next to me, Saran had his fingers crossed tightly.

After an eternity, Vandana shook his hand. 'I'm Vandana.'

'Oh, I know,' said Nikhil.

'What?' asked Vandana, sharply.

'I follow you on Twitter,' Nikhil admitted. 'You're @MissChiefManaged, aren't you?'

Vandana looked stumped. Nikhil gave her a lazy grin.

'You're really popular on Twitter! My friends know about you.'

'I had no idea,' Vandana mumbled, looking down at her feet. Her ears were turning red, but she sounded pleased.

'Oh yeah, yeah,' nodded Nikhil. 'I remember some of your tweets, too. That thing about rainforests or something?'

Vandana's face lit up. 'About people who protest against deforestation holding up signs made of paper? Ridiculous!'

Nikhil laughed. 'That's the one.' He cleared his throat slightly. 'So, uh, Saturday?'

'Absolutely,' Vandana smiled.

'Hockey grounds?' they said in unison, and laughed casually.

I didn't need to look at Saran's face to know he was smiling like a clown.

Nikhil's mother dragged Abhi by the arm, chiding him for disappearing into the Crime section. With a tiny smile at Vandana, Nikhil walked away with his family. Vandana shouldered her bag, its surviving contents restored, and strolled away in the direction of the busy main road again.

'Well done, kiddo,' I said to Saran.

He nodded happily, and hugged me. I couldn't explain why he felt warm, or why I could even feel it. But it was nice. The shards of glass and splashes of blobby jam lay forgotten.

❦

Saran sank into the pavement. He tore the bright red cap off his head, and I had to shield my eyes from his lurid hair to avoid being blinded.

'Could you put that cap back on?'

Saran crumpled the cap and stuffed it into his jeans.

'Why?'

'Because I like my corneas.'

'Fine, in deference to your corneas,' he said, putting it back on, 'I shall oblige you.'

We just sat there for a few minutes, without saying a word to each other. It wasn't awkward; I guess we both needed a moment's silence. Then, all at once, we launched into speech.

'That was awesome! Did you see her face?'

'I wish I could've clicked a picture!'

'He seems nice...'

'Waste of jam. It's a shame.'

'That was a huge can of pepper spray...'

'She likes Lee Child, wow.'

'I aced this test.'

'*Lee Child*!'

Saran gave his feet a satisfied smile, and clapped mud and gravel off his hands. 'I guess my work here is done.'

But I wasn't done chatting with this boy just yet. 'Hang on, I've got a whole list of questions for you!'

Saran looked like he wanted to make a run for it, but

seemed to think better of it. Maybe he'd encountered aggressive ghosts before.

'Alright,' he said, crossing his legs. 'What is it you want to know?

'You said the word fate like it was a person.'

'I don't hear a question.'

I grimaced. 'Why did you say the word fate like it was a real person?'

Saran smiled a little amusedly. 'Don't you think Fate could be a human wearing clothes and a pair of Fastrack sunglasses?'

'I think I'd belong in an asylum if I did,' I responded.

'Well,' Saran said, stretching the word, 'Fate's real. As is Destiny, Hope, Faith ...'

'Yeah, yeah, I get the picture,' I said impatiently. I frowned at the ground. 'What did you say to Nikhil to bring him back?'

Saran shrugged.

'I told him his brother was stuck inside, wailing for his mommy.'

'But how come they walked away without him in the first place?'

Another shrug, this one with a mischievous grin.

'A happy accident, I guess. Things clicked into place, right? I wouldn't have had a sound reason to drag Nikhil back to Blossom's if he hadn't forgotten his brother.'

I grinned at the convenient coincidence.

'Next question.' Saran prompted.

I caught hold of my wispy pants and twisted them into a knot.

'How come you readily agreed to my suggestion of hitching Nikhil with Vandana instead of Countess Dracula?'

Saran scratched his chin.

'The conviction in your voice. You said that this was a boy you loved, and yet, there you were, finding him someone who'd actually make him happy. That takes a lot of bravery, doesn't it? Only cowards holds on to things which they cannot have. You were strong. And I supposed that your determination and strength came from true conviction, and a desire to let go.'

I stared at him in wonder.

'Who *are* you? How do you...' I struggled to find words. 'How is it that someone like you,' I gestured at the dirty jeans and green hair, 'is so impossibly wise?'

'I'm a happy little accident, I guess,' Saran said with a tiny wink.

'Why do you keep saying that? A happy... accident...' I trailed off.

Cause an accident.

My back pocket seemed to grow heavier. I'd completely forgotten about my last task. I swore loudly.

'By the arrow of Cupid, lower your voice!' Saran yelped, shielding his ears.

'Sorry,' I said hastily. 'I was supposed to do something, and I completely forgot about it.'

'What is it?' frowned Saran.

The very notion of sharing my troubles with Saran seemed laughable. But he prodded me.

'Go on.'

I drew in a shuddering breath. 'I have to cause an accident, as awful as that sounds. *Roads paved with jam,* if I'm quoting my...question paper...verbatim.'

Saran gaped at me.

'You're astonishingly slow, aren't you?' Shaking his head at my confused expression, Saran bade me follow him to Blossom's again. I was starting to feel bored of going back and forth.

'What do you see?' he asked.

'Assorted novels,' I said immediately, quite forgetting that this was not a competitive quiz.

'On the road, dummy.'

I looked down. Covering a small stretch of about a foot, was the sheet of bright red mixed-fruit jam from Vandana's bag.

'Jam...' I said slowly.

'Very good, 10 points to you,' Saran said, while slow-clapping me. 'Now, what caused it?'

I didn't answer immediately. I didn't need further patronising from Saran.

'Vandana's collision with Nikhil. Bag split, stuff everywhere, jam fell to the floor.'

Saran mimed wiping a proud tear from his eyes. 'That's my girl! Now, what do you call that collision?'

Something clicked in my head.

'An accident.'

I gazed at Saran in wonder.

'You're welcome,' he winked.

'But... how?'

Saran's eyes sparkled with so much mischief that it was quite hard to look into them without feeling the urge to prank everyone in my phonebook while also wishing them well. 'Think.'

'They collide by mistake, but it brings them together. A happy accident,' I said. 'Wow! I completed my task! Wait... Who are you?'

The boy smiled very, very mischievously. And his smile acted like a trigger for spontaneous change. His hair turned from bright green to caramel brown and finally to black. A small ponytail popped into sight. His dirty clothes were replaced by a leather jacket. A bow and arrow appeared in his hands and hard boots appeared on his feet. I took in the frame of the very man I'd seen during my walk with the Middler.

'I'm Sarandip,' he said. 'People also know me as Serendipity, but that's a bit of a mouthful, isn't it? My father is Cupid, and my mother is an Imp from Hell. That would explain the juxtaposition of good and bad in my personality. I know what you're thinking—how do I look this young?'

I was thinking about a hundred things, but that wasn't it. But Saran was still talking.

'I think it's the immortality. I can turn myself into whatever I want, being partly divine and darkly powerful. It's a perk that comes with the job. It's a hard job, mine. I like these benefits, though. They really keep me going. For instance, I can see ghosts.' He waved a hand at me. 'I can't Possess people, but that's okay, I'd suffer in a body that wasn't my own. I prefer Morphing to Possessing, really.'

My mind raced. No wonder he'd seemed so familiar. Now that he mentioned it, the family resemblance was uncanny. Those mildly gentle yet mischievous eyes had been passed on from father to son. My voice returned feebly.

'You are really... Serendipity?'

'Yes, yes, I am,' Saran said.

I gulped down a few pointless questions and went with, 'Where's that chariot of yours?'

'Oh,' Saran waved a hand. 'I parked it inside a mall. Made it visible and everything, so now people in there are trying to win it by participating in some contest.'

'And the Rolls?'

Saran sighed. 'Still out of commission, I'm afraid. Maddy's not going to like that,' he muttered more to himself than to me.

'Er, Maddy?' I asked.

'Maddy! Oh, come now, you've met him!' Saran looked surprised. 'You were walking with him when I met you on your way to the Commons!'

My voice went weak. 'The Middler's name is Maddy?'

'Well, Madhav, but my brother's always preferred Maddy,' said Saran.

I wished there was some way to filter news snippets so they could fill into my lap at intervals much longer than these. It would make the digestion process a lot easier. 'You're the Middler's *brother*?' I squeaked.

'Well, yes.' Saran looked suddenly awkward. 'See, our father, Cupid, he's rather charming, as you can imagine. Eons ago, he developed an inconvenient habit of spawning with multiple Imps. Never Angels. Because that would be inappropriate, you understand, what with us being family and all. Anyway, he had twins with one Imp named Camilla.'

'Uh huh,' I said. 'Sure, sure.'

'Anyway, Maddy and I were born. Fraternal twins. Father always favoured me more. He always liked a talkative kid. So, I ended up with the better everything. Larger piece of cake, better bicycle, nicer job. Maddy hates his job. He's been stuck in it for—'

'—fifteen millenia, yeah, he told me,' I said.

'He's nice... Maddy,' said Saran, shaking his head. 'He ought to loosen up a bit, that's all. Father doesn't hate him, mind you. He actually misses him, hasn't seen him in ages, and he desperately wants to. Maddy doesn't think he's anything to us.'

Something in Saran's jacket beeped and he checked a

small phone.

'Duty calls!' he said. 'I should be off. I shall have to take your leave, Arundathi. It was a pleasure!'

I found my voice again. 'So you really are Serendipity, then?'

'Ah, the slow transition from shock to denial to reluctant belief. I'm afraid I cannot witness the happy process. I do have other TSOCs to execute.' He looked at me with kind eyes. 'Arundathi, those who help me often help themselves. If you still are in any doubt of this, check your aura. That much gold is quite admirable.'

And with a tiny wave of his hand, Serendipity popped out of sight, leaving me alone outside Blossom's, with nothing more than astonishment mingled with the scent of mixed-fruit jam.

8

Anger Mismanagement

I kept staring at the spot where Saran had disappeared. I was still reeling.

Momentarily forgetting that I still had more than half a Checklist to complete, I asserted my rights to total absent-mindedness, and wandered around the city for a while.

The thing about Bangalore is that it never fails to surprise you. Just when you've got used to a smooth stretch of tar, a pothole cracks up. And it's not even those nice potholes which lead you to parallel universes with fairies and dragons and jalebi fields. I'm talking about the ones that are capable of tripping up even monster trucks.

And then there are the people. You just expect to swim through a sea of software engineers, and more often than not you do. But then there's that one guy who has a bachelor's degree in Arts in that sludge. A unicorn in a jungle of zebras. You can recognize this chap easily because he's the only one who wouldn't be able to converse in the local language of Python.

There's also the sweet surprise of finding a bit of jaggery in your sambar. My friends from Chennai never appreciated this, though. For them, Bangalore sambar belonged in a confectionery store. It was OK, though, I felt. What's wrong with a little—'AIEEE!'

Something was pulling me from behind! I tried to look over my shoulder but I couldn't turn. I felt like my powers had been sapped. I was no longer in control of my body.

I panicked and jerked my shoulders and stretched my neck, hoping to break free. But it was of no use. My eyes screwed tight against the wind, I zoomed backwards by almost a kilometre. Finally, the sharp sensation in my lower back faded and I collapsed into a mountain of mud emptied near a construction site.

''bout time, I've been lookin' everywhere for you,' said a gruff voice.

I heard heavy footsteps approaching me. Too afraid to see anything, I kept my eyes tightly shut.

'Get outta there, I don' 'ave all day,' the voice commanded.

I gulped. The mud passed through my throat, and although I couldn't actually inhale it, I coughed on instinct. Reluctantly, I opened my eyes by a fraction. I was seeing double—double tree, double overflowing dustbin, double stray dog. And double guy-with-evil-look-on-face.

I groaned.

If I had a rupee for every time I got abducted by an Imp from Hell ... well, I'd be a rupee richer, I thought weakly to myself before I passed out.

❦

Dingy alleys in Bangalore are few and far between. Or so I used to think.

As it turns out, there are at least thirty alleys in the Matthikere area alone where one can contribute to the booming drug trade or beat up innocents for money; or cower over ghosts and threaten to blow their brains out.

The Imp removed two fingers from the side of my head. I stood my ground.

'You realize that I can't die *again*, right?' I said blandly to the dim-witted Imp.

He stepped obscenely close to me, thrusting his face within an inch of mine. I tried not to gag—he smelled like a public toilet or an open drain or a lunch box that has been opened after two days inside a school bag. He was lean and muscular, with a clichéd skull tattoo at the side of his neck. His eyes were mean slits in a face about as attractive as a blowfish.

'You bein' clever w'th me?' he asked menacingly.

I frowned. 'Why do you have that accent? Sounds really fake.'

The Imp growled softly.

Antagonizing an Imp with powers to render ghosts unconscious was not the brightest idea I'd produced all day. I hastily aimed for damage control.

'Um, what's your name?'

'Rakesh,' he grunted, and puffs of smoke issued from his nostrils. 'But everyone calls me Rocky.' He stuck out his chest proudly, as if the name usually reserved for pet Alsatians was inexpressibly flattering.

I suppressed a smirk. 'Nice. Are you an Imp?'

'One o' the meanest,' he grinned, and spat on the ground to show just how mean an Imp he was.

I offered him a deeply impressed look. I had used it every time someone started bragging about their achievements like winning first place in a local quiz contest or new levels scaled in Candy Crush Saga.

'Wow, you must be pretty accomplished to have pulled me all over that distance,' I said, my voice as greasy as his hair.

Rocky's grin widened. Clearly, playing to someone's ego, even if they were thick-skulled beasts from the Underworld, always worked.

'You don' know nothin' 'bout my powers, girly,' he grunted. 'They come in all forms. I can lift mountains and toss 'em far, if I wanna.'

'Sure, sure,' I said, nodding. 'I mean, if you wanna do somethin', you *totally* gotta.'

The Imp was too slow to understand that I was making fun of him. In fact, if he were any slower, he'd achieve the average pace of Bangalore's rush hour traffic.

While the Imp was busy figuring out my mockery, I scouted my peripherals to gauge for an escape route hidden in the squalid filth. The ground was littered with garbage and earthworms. A deflated truck tyre lay behind me, cockroaches and miscellaneous creepy-crawlies scuttling all over it. But the moss-covered wall on my right…it seemed easy enough to pass through. Maybe, just maybe, it could be my exit strategy.

'You makin' fun o' me?' roared the Imp, finally.

'What?' I hurriedly pulled a face of innocence. 'No way! How mad do you think I am? I'd rather eat these earthworms than mock such a powerful Imp!'

Rocky grunted, seemingly satisfied with the lie.

His brain seemed to be constructing his next thought. This is it, I told myself. Make your move, Arundathi.

I clapped my hands and brightened my eyes, preparing to make a run, or rather fly, for it.

'Well, it's been absolutely spiffing to have met you, Mr Rocky. I think I'll just, you know—'

I leapt up, and made to squeeze into the wall to my right, but the Imp was as quick as a flash. In a second, he had me pinned against the wall.

'Let—go—of—me,' I croaked.

'Think I'm stupid, girly?' he breathed. 'I've battled Imps

and Angels all my life. Whatcha gonna do, huh? Think you can mess with me? ME?'

He shoved me away, and I slumped to the floor. I glared up at him with burning eyes.

'Master Satan has sent me 'ere on an important mission, and I'd rather jump into the Holy Pool than botch it up,' he said, his voice raspy.

'What do you want from me?' I demanded.

A horrible smile spread across Rocky's lips, reminding me of the Joker from the Batman series.

'Anger. Rage. Fury. Wrath. I want it all.' He licked his lips almost lasciviously. 'I want you to summon every bit o' hatred you can and spit it out in the form o' words. Throw 'em like pots an' pans. Hurl 'em like cannonballs. Shoot 'em like bullets. Do whatever you can to get really, really angry. I want that aura o' yours to turn extra red.'

He paused for effect.

'I'm the Chief o' Rage and Anger Provokers 'ere on Operation Red Colour.'

Great, I thought as I sunk into the corner of the dark alley. Now I have to deal with the CRAP on ORC.

❦

'Royal Challengers Bangalore is the worst team.'

'I hear they're pretty bad these days, yeah.'

'Death bowling? More like dead bowling!'

'If you say so.'

'Get angry!'

'No, shan't.' I said, shrugging my shoulders with boredom.

'AAARGH!'

I sighed as Rocky kicked the wall. I didn't even flinch. The only thing making me slightly edgy was the fact that the sun had set and I still hadn't checked the scroll for my next task. This blithering idiot of an Imp was wasting my time. He'd needled me for more than three hours, and hadn't touched a single nerve.

And now, he was using cricket to infuriate me. It was a sport I had scant interest in. What was so captivating about a Test match, I'd never truly understood. The stupidest thing Rocky was doing was to get me to defend a cricket team whose most significant achievement was forcing its players into jerseys that were so bright that they could be seen from Jupiter.

'Curse RCB, come on!' bellowed Rocky, shaking his fists at me.

I yawned widely, and shook my head.

Rocky's eyes were bloodshot. His breathing was heavy, and a vein near his temple looked ready to burst any second. He fell silent, and crouched a few feet from me, pulling out a gadget as he did.

'Background,' he barked into it, and flipped it shut.

The creases on my forehead betrayed my curiosity, and

Rocky smiled in a satisfied sort of way. A few minutes passed in silence.

'Beep!'

The phone in Rocky's pocket sounded, and he read the message, his lips moving soundlessly. The text seemed to contain words with more than three syllables because he kept going back several times. Finally, he put the phone away, and stood over me with his most intimidating look yet.

'Let's talk about your parents,' he said softly.

I froze.

'What?' My voice sounded hollow.

'Your parents,' the Imp repeated. 'You know, your mother an' your father. The couple o' doctors up in Indiranagar, with the fancy car, an' the bungalow, an', oh, another kid. Your parents who...'

'Shut up,' I said quietly.

The Imp grinned evilly because he knew, and I knew, he'd succeeded.

There are certain events that influence feelings, thoughts and personalities, commit themselves to memory so strongly that you can remember every single detail. As a child growing up, I'd never really believed in the power of these events, or even that they might one day change my life.

Oh, how very wrong I'd been.

It was the inter-school Spelling Bee. I was thirteen years old then, and the boy I had just lost to—Aditya—was a year or two younger than me, perhaps. My eyes were burning with tears, but I managed to smile at him and shake hands. And though my vision was blurred by tears, I couldn't help but notice the similarities between him and me—the same off-centre nose, the same lopsided smile, thick, slanted eyebrows and just our general appearance. We even shared a surname, I noticed, as my eyes fell on his name tag.

Aditya's mother came along and showered him with hugs and kisses, and I just stood there awkwardly staring at the ground. Just then, my grandmother came to my side, beaming with pride. 'Second place, Aru. Chin up!' She gave me a brief hug and straightened. Still smiling, her eyes fell on Aditya and his mother, who was busy straightening her son's tie and didn't look up.

For some unfathomable reason, my grandmother's arms stiffened. I could feel the sudden force of her tightened grip on my shoulders.

'Let's go,' she said sharply, and grabbed my hand.

'But... what? Why?' I started to protest, but my grandmother was already dragging me away from the auditorium. Soon, we were out on the streets, hailing an autorickshaw back home.

Past experience had taught me never to pester my grandmother when she was staring determinedly at her feet with her hands balled into fists in her lap. I remained silent.

Dinner that night was a quiet affair. I was still sour about having lost the Spelling Bee and about my grandmother's sullenness.

'His last name was Ramachandran, too,' I said, finally breaking my silence. 'Aditya. The kid who won.'

My grandmother kept her eyes fixed on her plate.

'Even his mother looked a lot like me. Isn't that weird?' I asked.

I noticed my grandmother gulp. Beads of sweat dotted her nose like they always did when she was nervous.

'You know them, somehow, don't you?' I persisted. 'You went all stiff when you saw them together.'

My grandmother shifted in her seat. I rose from mine and kneeled down next to her.

'What is it that you're not telling me?' I asked her quietly.

When she looked at me, her face was lined deeper than ever before. She looked pained. It frightened me, made me anxious.

'I'm so sorry, Aru,' she whispered.

We sat down in the living room.

'Remember how your aunt told you about a car crash that…' she started to say.

'…killed my parents, yeah,' I interjected. 'What about it?'

My grandmother closed her eyes and said, 'There was no car crash.'

The rest of her story turned my heart to stone.

My parents hadn't died in a road accident. It wasn't, as my close relatives had pretended for years, a miracle that I'd survived the crash, for there had been no crash to survive.

'I don't understand,' I said, my voice sounding small and distant.

My grandmother sighed. 'Your parents met a long time ago. They were in college together, and they fell for each other. I knew it. Your blessed aunt knew it. But what we didn't know, was that your parents... they... did something stupid one night. A mistake. The kind you cannot erase without suffering great anguish.'

My mother was nineteen years old when she'd become pregnant with me. She'd dropped out of college, had me, and barely a few weeks after I came unexpectedly into the world, she'd left me in my grandmother's arms, and left, never to return home again.

'My daughter, your mother... she was distraught, Aru, you must understand that,' said my grandmother, as gently as she could. 'She didn't want to leave you, but she insisted she had to, for your own good.'

She went away to a different city with my father and started their life anew. They got married and had a boy soon. My grandmother started to tell me that it wasn't the worst thing in the world, but I never found out why she felt that way because I'd fled the room and thrown myself onto my bed, crying my eyes out. Everything had been a lie. Everything I'd been told, I'd believed, I'd lived through. It was just one big lie.

That night, I'd barely slept. I'd lain on my back with a numb feeling. The only thought that kept repeating itself was that my parents had been petrified at the thought of having me, but somehow, completely at ease with disposing me. They hadn't so much as named me when they'd placed me in my grandmother's care. All I had was the last name.

I spent years carefully bottling my emotions and dodging family-related questions which casually sprung up in conversations. I never spoke of this incident again. Not to my friends, nor to my grandmother, nor to my family. I felt ashamed, angry, betrayed. My parents were horrible people. They didn't deserve a minute's thought. I shoved them into a deep recess of my mind, and seldom visited it. But now, I found myself in the dark recess again, much against my will.

Rocky's teeth gleamed in the dark alley.

'Talk, girly.'

I remained silent.

The Imp paced up and down, his eyes fixed on mine. He looked like a tiger playing with its prey before it pounced on it.

'Why did they leave? Didn't lurve you enough?' he taunted.

I stared determinedly at the ground. A worm was digging its way into the earth, puncturing the hard mud with all its might.

'You musta bin a real loser baby, right? Not cute enough, probably. Musta really sucked to 'ave' had you in the first place, like.'

Don't rise to the bait, Arundathi, don't rise, I intoned. It's exactly what he wants. But to my dismay, I could feel my composure fading. It must've shown in my face because I could feel my cheeks flush.

'Oh, come on,' Rocky wheedled, his voice horribly sweet now. 'Can't be tha' bad. They just abandoned—'

SMACK!

I slapped the Imp hard across the face. I didn't even register that I had actually made physical contact with flesh, but I immediately waited for an ugly retaliation.

Rocky looked as if Diwali had come early.

'Oooh, I like this.'

'Shut up,' I repeated, with my barely controlled anger.

'You're gettin' there, almost…' said the Imp with great relish.

'Leave me alone!' I yelled, covering my face with my hands.

The Imp forced my hands apart and peered at me with eyes full of mock-concern. For five whole seconds, he said nothing. Then, 'Is tha' wha' you said to your parents, too?'

A terrible, white-hot anger bubbled inside me. I raised my head, my nostrils flaring like a raging bull's. Before I could stop myself, I was bellowing at the top of my lungs.

'NO! ALRIGHT? MY PARENTS DIDN'T NEED *ME* TO TELL THEM TO LEAVE! THEY DIDN'T NEED ANYONE! THEY DIDN'T WANT ME! THEY DIDN'T CARE! THEY DESERTED ME THE

MINUTE I WAS BORN! I WAS TOSSED ASIDE LIKE GARBAGE!'

I hadn't spoken about this for years, and now, the dam had broken. I was trembling with apoplectic rage.

'THEY WERE YOUNG WHEN THEY HAD ME, I BELIEVE! THEY LEFT ME WITH MY GRANDMOTHER! LUCKY *SHE* DIDN'T CHUCK ME, RIGHT? LIKE IT MATTERED THAT SHE HAD TAKEN ME IN, I'M *DEAD*!'

The Imp's lips were curved in a smile so wide it made me angrier still.

'They haven't once visited me, not once! They're so happy with their *precious* boy now, aren't they? They had him two *years* after I came into the world. People really do change in that amount of time, right? Twenty is too young for a baby, but twenty-two is fan-bloody-tastic!'

My ears were burning now. I began to laugh a little hysterically. Years of pent up anger was cascading out of me, and it didn't look pretty.

'Obviously, I was too much of a burden. Who needs a girl, anyway? It's not like I would've done any heavy lifting the boys are capable of. Maybe if I was a boy, right? WRONG! They just didn't *want* me! TO HELL WITH THEM!'

I sank to my knees and yelled until my voice turned hoarse. Hot, angry tears rolled down my cheeks before I could stop them. For a while, I couldn't stop. I felt faint, tired and horribly weak. I longed to throw things, smash them. But I couldn't.

Minutes later, when I'd stopped banging the ground with my ineffectual fists, the Imp took a few steps towards me. His face was etched with a hugely satisfied look.

'Tha' was wicked, the way you shouted your lungs out. Excellent work. Bravo,' he patted me on the shoulder. 'I hope we get the chance to work together, sometime. Goin' by your aura right now, I think we will.' He gave me the thumbs up.

I reluctantly glanced at my aura, and felt my stomach lurch. It was a sphere of red. No gold in sight. Not the slightest tinge. Ten minutes of intense rage and bitterness, and I'd blown every bit of good I'd done so far.

I lowered my gaze, only to find that the Imp was gone. His job was complete, and I was alone in the quiet dark.

❦

A lamp glowed dimly in the living room. Its light fell on a grandfather clock standing by the wall, casting long, dark shadows across the mosaic flooring. The dining table was scrubbed clean, and mats were placed at four corners, with steel tumblers and spoons on them. Everything looked so neat and tidy.

I circled around the balcony and went over to a smaller room next to the kitchen. A desk stood by a corner, littered with crumpled sheets of paper, sharpened pencils, and a tangled mess of headphones. The bed was made, but scarves and belts lay strewn upon it, making it look like a bumper sale in cheap polyester and faux leather. A dreamcatcher hung carelessly on the wall, looking very much as if it was still there only because it had been a gift, and it would've been rude to have recycled it into confetti. Comic books were stacked neatly on a tiny bookshelf by the door, and they were the only things inside the room that looked as if they were truly cared for.

I soared into my room. My grandmother had been in to clean it, evidently; the floor didn't have bits of paper or balled up socks. For the first time since the dark alley, I smiled.

The same smile faded when my eyes fell on the large poster of the movie *Fight Club* on one of the walls. The unholy moustache that Rishi had drawn with a green marker on Brad Pitt's face was still visible. It would've made a wonderful advertisement for Pinkin's Permanent Markers Company, I thought sourly.

I squinted at the poster, and something that had eluded my outrage for six years caught my eye. Right at the bottom of the poster, in the same green ink as the moustache, were the words 'Marla Singer, you make my heart sing', in Rishi's untidy scrawl. (That guy was destined for a career in Medicine.) I read the words again and cringed. Rishi was hopeless.

Sitting down on my bed, I took a deep breath. Then with each consequent breath, a sense of hopelessness threatened to engulf me, but it only took one look at the photograph of my grandmother on my bedside table to remind me that I should not give up. If only my grandmother knew how persuasive she could be even without a rolling pin in her hand.

I unrolled the Checklist. When I finished reading God's next task for me, my jaw was set. I knew exactly what I had to do.

Straightening, I approached my writing desk, let myself into a sheet of paper, and set myself down on the wooden surface. Slowly, I chose a pen to write with, and entered it. Sitting pretty inside a beautiful red Parker with royal blue ink coursing through me, I began to write. On more than one occasion, I had to pause to rephrase, but I didn't completely stop until I had written everything I wanted to say.

It was midnight when I finally finished writing. Making sure everything was exactly as I'd found it (I didn't want to spook my grandmother), I flew out of the pen.

Without so much as a glance at the Checklist, I rolled on to my bed and fell asleep.

9

Ghost Post

I woke up to the smell of filter coffee. Rich, strong, perfectly brewed filter coffee. I could almost taste the beverage. Flinging my legs off the bed, I swooped into the kitchen, not stopping to consider what the sight of my grandmother would do to my already fragile emotions.

There she was, standing at the stove, spooning sugar into a steel tumbler filled to the brim with foamy goodness. A terrible joy and a terrible sadness collided inside me. It was like the two emotions were battling for my attention. I simply wafted forward as if in a trance, and unblinkingly threw my arms around my grandmother. Her warmth was intoxicating.

I was careful not to accidentally Possess her. I couldn't afford to mess up her soul. It wouldn't do it if her thoughts and memories got rearranged—what would the world be without her filter coffee?

I let go (after too short a minute) and followed her out

of the kitchen, all the way into the living room. Everything was orderly and tidy. It was just like my grandmother to keep the house spick and span, come rain or shine.

My grandmother sat down on the sofa and sipped her coffee with her chestnut-brown eyes out of focus. I stared at her for as long as she drank, and even as she flipped through the thin sheets of *The Hindu*. She tutted as she spotted a poorly framed sentence somewhere. A college degree in English Literature had permitted her to enjoy simple joys such as yelling 'Aha!' and pointing out errors in the local pages for several years now. She also took great pleasure in inking in the tiny squares of the crossword after I'd given up on it after just two cryptic hints.

I would've gladly spent an eternity watching my grandmother live out her life, but time and tide stopped for no man, let alone a ghost with a messed-up aura. This was my last day on earth, and the Checklist wasn't going to extend its deadline. Any delay would only serve to damn me.

I hurried into my room. Taking a deep breath, I whooshed into the sheet.

The urge to turn into a paper plane and fly about the house was overwhelming, but I had a feeling my grandmother would think herself insane if she were to see a paper plane flying by itself along the length and breadth of the living room. And I couldn't bring myself to be responsible for the loss of my grandmother's grandchild *and* sanity within the same week.

I folded myself into an envelope, with the words facing outwards so my grandmother would not regard it as rubbish. Falling flat on the floor, I began my slow journey across the old mosaic tiles. The flooring was bursting with memories—my first steps as a chubby toddler; my tantrums involving the beating of my fists on the ground; my accidental spilling of oil resulting in my grandmother's hip bidding goodbye to intactness.

A few minutes later, I reached my grandmother's foot. She was about to rise from the sofa when a gust of wind blew in from the window behind me, flattening me against her ankle.

The sheet grazed bare skin and my grandmother looked down, her forehead creased. The gold bangles on her hand jingled as her slim, wrinkled fingers circled around the sheet's corners. I flew out of the paper just as she began to unfold the improvised envelope. She clapped a hand to her mouth when she read the first two words—

Dearest Grannazi,

It was my pet name for her; a juvenile amalgamation of the words granny and grammar nazi. She'd loved it.

She read on, aloud but softly.

I hope you are—

But just then, the doorbell rang loudly, startling my grandmother into dropping the letter. Even I jumped. Who would come calling at seven in the morning? The milkman and newspaper boy had already come and gone. Was it the annoying flower lady who tried to sell us wilted jasmines?

My grandmother walked slowly to the door and looked through the peephole while I tried to see through the gap between the door and the floor. Only a pair of chappals met my eyes. Above me, my grandmother sighed exasperatedly and reluctantly pulled the door open after arranging her features to a more amicable expression.

I groaned when I saw who stood at the doorstep. Of course; how could I have forgotten? Meera aunty. This particular neighbour had made a habit out of enjoying a large tumbler of my grandmother's coffee every morning, while regaling her with what she assumed was priceless gossip.

'Good morning!' she boomed, flinging her chappals to one side of the doorstep.

My grandmother gave her a weak smile in return. This semi-friendly gesture was more than enough for Meera aunty to let herself into the house. Like a wobbly, infant gorilla, she trudged past the shoe rack, and threw herself on the sofa. The old springs creaked in protest.

'Come and sit, Savithri aunty, it is your house!' She patted the sofa.

My grandmother, resigned to the fate of yet another lost morning, joined her. I followed suit, with a sour expression on my face.

Meera aunty's piggy eyes scanned the teapoy. 'Oh, you had coffee already? I thought I will have with you. It's OK,

I will invite myself over to Akhila aunty's house for coffee today. Ha ha ha.'

I stared stonily at her. She looked particularly unpleasant today, her enormous form squashed into a revolting blue nightie. Most of her ample neck was covered by a yellowing towel—a makeshift dupatta that did more harm to fashion than bell-bottom jeans ever had.

'Why didn't you come walking today?' asked Meera aunty, plucking at the corners of her towel.

'I didn't feel like it,' answered my grandmother shortly.

'You are just like my husband,' she barked conversationally. 'Lazy man never comes with me. Says he has work. What work? God alone knows!'

Maybe he looks forward to those precious twenty minutes of Meera-free solitude? I began my internal monologue.

'He doesn't even let me go anywhere! I say to him, the other day, "Giridhar, I'm heading to the club with Pranjali," and he says, "Not alone! I'll also come!" I mean, for God's sake, let me go alone, na?' Meera aunty pouted. She looked like an overgrown baby.

'How is Giri?' my grandmother asked, feigning interest in Meera aunty's ball and chain.

'High cholesterol!' wailed Meera aunty, a palm on her head. 'He eats only my cooking every day, but still he has high cholesterol.'

You make potato-fry every day. It's a wonder his heart

hasn't exploded yet.

'Maybe you shouldn't make so much potato-fry every day, Meera,' my grandmother suggested.

Ha! Thank you!

'What will we eat, then? Fish food?' demanded Meera aunty.

Seeing as you've reached the size of a killer whale, it is recommended, yes.

'I'm telling you, Meera...' my grandmother began, but Meera aunty cut her short.

'Leave it, aunty. Why am I sharing these troubles with you?'

Yes, why indeed.

'I'll tell you some juicy titbits I heard from Latha.'

Oh, I'm giddy with excitement now.

And she dove into her usual dose of gossip.

'Deepti, that Harish's daughter, she has a boyfriend, it seems! Younger than her by *four months*! I was shocked. That girl always seemed so meek and mild. Who knew she was such a loose character? I will pray to Vishnu and Shiva, both! God only should save our apartment from this promiscuous witch!

'Sunil has got one car from his company. Basically he is getting paid less now, stupid fellow. I would have taken the money instead, and paid for his wife's nose surgery. It is so huge; no wonder she keeps poking it where it doesn't belong.'

She went on for what felt like an hour. I woke from the

reverie when I suddenly heard my name.

'...for our Arundathi!'

When had she started claiming joint-ownership over me along with my grandmother? I was *their* Arundathi, now?

'Excuse me?' my grandmother said sharply. 'What did you ask Latha about Aru?'

'One nice boy, I had asked about,' Meera aunty said. 'You know, for marrying her off.'

I could've killed her. The audacity of this woman!

'His name is Arjun. Very nice boy,' Meera aunty continued, pleased at having captured my grandmother's full attention at last. 'Tall, handsome, jet black moustache. Engineer, obviously.'

Obviously. God forbid he was a talented dancer or a gifted violinist. Ugh, the horror.

'But then, by the time I spoke to Arjun's mother, Arundathi...' Meera Aunty trailed off.

My grandmother shifted on the sofa.

'Sorry, I shouldn't have said anything,' said Meera aunty hastily. But that didn't mean that she'd stop.

Yes, maybe you shouldn't have.

'But, Aunty, if you don't mind my asking—'

SHE DOES! SHE DOES! SHE DOES!

'—why did you let Arundathi go outside with those *boys* that night? She is...was a *girl*.'

She'd gone too far.

'Out.' My grandmother's voice was soft but firm.

'Yes, yes, out,' Meera aunty nodded vigorously. 'Why did you let her go out?'

Good God, you are thick as your neck, woman.

My grandmother rose to her feet and gave Meera aunty a look of loathing she had only ever reserved for badly-set curd.

'Get out of my house this instant!'

A curtain of confusion and shock dropped over Meera aunty's face.

'What are you saying, Aunty? Are you suffering from dementia?'

Dementia isn't quantifiable. Also, GET OFF MY PROPERTY, YOU NIGHTIE-FLAUNTING GORILLA MASQUERADING AS A WOMAN!

'I'm saying,' said my grandmother, slowly and deliberately, 'if you don't leave my house right this second, I will call the watchman and ask him to set his dog on you.'

Meera aunty looked as if she'd been punched on the nose. 'I've never been this insulted!' she shrieked.

'I thought insult was something you were quite accustomed to,' said my grandmother coolly. 'And don't bother coming back here for another cup of coffee!'

Meera aunty huffed and muttered heatedly.

'And *you* don't expect anything from me, crazy old lady!'

She pushed herself to her feet and heaved her bulk out of the door with much difficulty.

My grandmother shut the door behind her.

'...talking about *my* granddaughter...drinking up all the *Cothas*...idiot woman...'

I could've kissed her. Beaming, I sat down next to her on the sofa as she retrieved the letter from the floor and began to read again.

Dear Grannazi,

I hope you are reading this in the privacy of our home, without Meera aunty's eyes boring into the letter.

My grandmother grinned.

I have three things to tell you, and funnily enough, they're all made up of three words. Without further ado, here goes.

I'm a moron.

Remember that time I came back home with a wound on my knee, and told you I'd just tripped and fallen on the road? I lied. I reversed my scooter extremely fast out of the parking lot, skided, and grazed my knee on a brick wall. I could've got it treated, but I almost fainted at the thought of the dispensary. So, I just raced home. That's how I got the scar. Something tells me you saw right through my lie, so, moving on.

I failed Kannada.

In the eighth standard! It was a long time ago, alright? I didn't show you my test paper, because it would have given you a heart attack. And I didn't want you to die, so

I just forged your signature. Besides, you have to forgive me now, because like I said, it was a long time ago, and there is a statute of limitation on these things.

Here's the third thing. Brace yourself.

I love you.

I really, truly do. You are the most amazing woman I know. You make the best Mysore Pak! (Honestly, how on earth do you get it to melt like that? Genius!) You speak English better than the English, you dance like no one's watching (even though Meera aunty undoubtedly is), and you are as sweet as that chocolate tea we bought in Ooty (Remember that? It was so yummy). You've given me a lifetime of happiness.

Grandmother. Father. Mother. Sibling. Best friend. For being all this and more, thank you.

(I can't believe I started writing this six months ago, and finished it only now! You're allowed to curse me for this laziness.)

Forever yours,
Aru

My grandmother's hands were shaking. I looked at her from the corner of my eye. It wasn't like my grandmother to get very emotional about death (she'd seen my grandfather and her sisters pass away), but on this occasion, she had succumbed to tears.

It wasn't something I wanted to see. She'd always been my rock. And I didn't want anything, not even my death, tarnishing that. I got to my feet. Planting a kiss on my grandmother's forehead, I whispered, 'I love you. And your Mysore Pak. Stay awesome.'

With that, I flew out the living room and into the world outside again.

❦

Write a letter to someone you love.

I watched with grim satisfaction as a small tick mark appeared against God's task. I didn't bother checking my aura. I had vowed not to do it until the very last task was over.

It was eight in the morning. A fine Sunday to kick some solid Checklist butt.

I stared at the scroll to see what Satan expected of me next, but his assignments seemed reluctant to show up, and the Checklist remained resolutely blank.

Ten minutes, twenty minutes, thirty minutes. Nothing. Spiky black letterage would appear haphazardly across the sheet, but just as quickly vanish. It was as if Satan couldn't make up his mind.

I was starting to panic. I felt like a student again, like there was the looming threat of a semester exam without any notes to go along.

I remembered how my friends and I used to cram for

exams in a basketball court a little away from my house. It was a nice place, full of trees and sunshine.

In a feeble attempt to calm my nerves, I took the shortest route to the basketball court a couple of kilometres from my apartment. I couldn't explain it, but I'd always experienced tranquillity at this place. It was strange that I did, considering that it was a haven for children and teenage boys armed with basketballs who were just waiting to give one a concussion. Even now, there was the danger that a ball might come flying at me and knock me senseless. But what were the odds of that happening now, anyway? Watching a ball soar right through my face might even help me cheer up.

The court was a secluded place which was visited by school kids in the mornings, and clingy lovers in the evenings (that was a totally different ball game). Today, it was occupied by noisy boys aged somewhere between eleven and fourteen years. They seemed to belong to a school team or one of those neighbourhood club teams, dressed in the same jerseys and shorts—bright yellow streaked with blue. An animal—a meerkat—was emblazoned across their chest. If the team wanted to look intimidating, it had failed miserably. I didn't know much about the logic behind choosing a mascot, but I was pretty sure that a meerkat wasn't exactly known for its ferocity.

Smirking slightly, I sat down on the highest step around the court and watched the boys argue about last morning's poor practice session.

'You didn't pass it to the right player!'

'Yes, I did! You just shut up, man! You're not even the captain!'

'Doesn't matter, you idiot. I told you not to pass to Rajeev, da!'

'But he was open!'

'JUST LIKE YOUR BIG FAT MOUTH!'

And they began to act like total idiots, kicking and punching each other. At one point, I saw someone's teeth make their mark on someone else's forearm. The only thing missing from this show was a cartoon anvil. If this had happened with girls, it would've got over in seconds—fake smiles and inward promises to stab each other in the back ten years from now.

I rolled my eyes at the bickering boys and sighed. Tranquillity wasn't on the cards here.

I was just about to leave when he entered the court, the last person I expected to see—Rishi.

I gaped, half-surprised, half-amused. Dressed in trousers, a black tie and a crisp white shirt, he was blending in with the basketball crowd as efficaciously as a duck would with a group of Swiss bankers.

I blinked twice to make sure it was really him. Nothing had changed; my old friend stood there at the far end of the court, carrying a stylish brown attaché.

I stared open-mouthed as he strode along the borders of the court and sat down not five feet from me.

A sudden, mischievous idea occurred to me. I took out the Middler's visibility necklace from my pocket. Creeping up right in front of Rishi, I held it in my hands.

Remember, I told the necklace, *I want to be seen only by Rishi, no one else. One, two, three!*

I threw the necklace around my neck. And sure enough—

'AAAAAAARGH!'

Rishi's ear-splitting yell attracted several stares from the boys on the court. Or so I hoped, because I couldn't really see anything. I had doubled over, clutching my stomach and howling with laughter.

'What's wrong?' a boy's voice came from somewhere behind me.

'Noth-nothing,' Rishi stammered, clutching his chest and breathing heavily as I lay inches from him, chuckling away to glory.

'Sure?' asked the boy.

'Yeah, yeah,' Rishi laughed nervously. 'Carry on with your game. It's all good!'

The sound of a bouncing basketball told me the boys had retreated. Chortling and snorting, I let myself up and looked at Rishi's panic-stricken face.

'What's up, Rishi?' I grinned. 'You look like you've seen a ghost.'

Rishi's face went, if possible, even whiter.

'Arundathi?'

I grinned wider still.

'But…you *died!*' cried Rishi.

I clicked my tongue in mock hurt. 'That's not a very nice thing to say.'

'Well… I…railway…the…' Rishi blubbered.

He took a deep breath.

'Is… Is it really you?'

'Larger than life, mister.'

'Very funny,' said Rishi, his voice already returning to its original snappish way. 'What the heck is happening?'

I sighed deeply.

'*That* is quite a tale. Got the time?'

'Got the beans?'

'Yeah.'

'Then spill them!'

'Er, here?' I looked around. A few of the basketball kids were still giving Rishi suspicious looks. 'You've got a group of pre-teens giving you funny looks because,' I quickly took off the necklace, 'you're talking to someone who isn't here.'

Rishi's took a swipe at me. A snigger escaped me and I put on the necklace again.

'Shall we head over to my house?' Rishi suggested.

I let surprise take over my expression. 'It's not even eight o'clock. Won't your parents be there?'

'They will,' Rishi replied bitterly. 'But I don't care.'

I gave him a sceptical look, and Rishi's answer revised itself considerably. 'OK, I do care, but we can let ourselves in through the back door.'

'Sure,' I grinned. 'All doors lead to home.'

'That's an unnecessary preposition,' Rishi pointed out immediately.

Banter failed me. But Rishi had beaten me fair and square. It was a moment reserved for dignified defeat. So, naturally, I stuck my tongue out and drenched the winner with spectral spit.

10

The Complicit Participant

Rishi's house was like any self-respecting bungalow—impossibly huge, with enough room to nest an entire village. A large garden embraced the mansion from all sides, with great orange hibiscuses swaying gently in the breeze. Three cars stood in the garage—a BMW, an Audi and a Volkswagen.

I walked through the fence and into the cobbled backyard.

'Hey, Rishi?' I said. 'Germany called. Wants all its cars back.'

Rishi merely rolled his eyes.

'Wow, poinsettias!' I said, looking at the bright red potted plants lining the path to the front door.

'That's what they're called?' Rishi said, a doltish expression on his face. 'I thought they were pirouettes or something!'

I was reminded of exactly why I so often referred to Rishi as an ape's bottom.

'Pirouettes are a ballet movement, numbskull.'

Rishi clicked his tongue. 'Like it matters.'

'You never told me your blood was blue,' I said, looking up at the spacious balconies.

Rishi threw a distasteful glance at the house. 'I'd rather live in a shack with no windows.'

'Ha-ha, you just described our college.'

The back door swung inwards without a sound, as we let ourselves into the house quietly.

'Welcome home,' said Rishi unenthusiastically, looking around to see if anyone was there.

We were near the empty dining area, with a view of the living room extension and a large TV room that was cut off from the rest of the house by delicate, beaded curtains.

Rishi grabbed a bottle of water from the fridge and motioned for me to follow him upstairs. There were photographs of his family all along the staircase, neatly framed and arranged chronologically. The baby Rishi seemed to be overly fond of chewing his bib while clutching his butt, while the adolescent Rishi seemed to be having a little trouble with facial hair (or lack of it thereof).

A huge family portrait hung near the landing right next to Rishi's room. The photograph was about as warm as an iceberg.

Rishi's father stood at the left, with a grim face and an intimidating handlebar moustache, towering over his family. Rishi's mother stood to the right, a mouse-faced woman with brown eyes and a sharp nose she'd passed on to the tall, gangly boy standing next to her and her husband.

'That's me,' Rishi said pointing to the boy, his remark as pointless as reality TV.

'Really?' I said. 'I couldn't have known at *all*!'

Rishi made a face and pushed open the door to his room. A shock of red nearly blinded me.

'What the...'

Every inch of wall was plastered with the same poster—that of the Spanish football team. I could see several smug faces grinning at me from the handsome mahogany cupboard.

'This is where the magic happens!' Rishi flung himself onto a bean bag.

'By magic, you mean the sudden disappearance of sight, yes?' I said, settling down on the bed.

'Excuse me?'

'What's with the red overdose? Did the Spanish dressing room throw up on your walls?'

'Hey, my parents let me decorate my own room the way I wanted!' Rishi protested.

'And in your infinite wisdom, you decide to do...this.' I applauded him sarcastically.

Rishi threw a cushion in my direction but it soared through the top of my head and landed on top of the desk.

'Being a ghost has its advantages,' I smirked.

'Speaking of which,' said Rishi, taking a sip of water, 'what happened after the accident? You're a ghost! HA! See? I *told* you, Arundathi! There are ghosts among us, you never once believed me! I was right all along!'

'Yeah, yeah, yeah,' I said, half-amused, half-exasperated.

'But how did you turn into a ghost?' frowned Rishi. 'Fill me in. Leave nothing out.'

I sighed. 'All right, fine. Story time.' I sat up a little straighter and cleared my throat. 'So, after I became railway-track paint—'

'Nice to see you have lost none of your charm,' Rishi grimaced.

I continued like he hadn't interrupted me. '—my soul bits sort of converged and I became a ghost. I couldn't feel anything, though. I was unconscious, see? Anyway, I took off and travelled to a purgatory-like place or some random place between Heaven and Earth. Then,' I suddenly brightened with a thought that hadn't struck me until now, 'I saw this freaky guy who looked like that first bencher. The one with the infinite supply of gel pens?'

'Nerd Nithin?' smirked Rishi.

'No, no, not him,' I said, snapping my fingers in impatience. 'The guy who sat next to him.'

'Abhishek!'

'Yes!' I laughed. Rishi joined in too, but I cut him off. 'Anyway, this half-red, half-golden fellow I met...'

I pulled Rishi into my thrilling tale, describing the

Middler, God and Satan, and even V, before diving into the mixed sceneries that had so befuddled me. I narrated how I'd been given three days to complete every task on the Checklist, which would determine whether I'd join God's or Satan's army.

'Was God pretty?' Rishi piped up at the end of my story.

'Are you serious?' I asked incredulously. 'Did you not hear me describe the garden with a split personality disorder?'

Rishi disregarded my words like he'd done for his entire Psychology syllabus last semester.

'That sounds like simple CGI. I want to know how God looks so I can have at least one thing to look forward to when I'm...'

'Dead?' I prompted. 'Napping in a graveyard? Getting your gut examined by vultures?'

'I was going to say "passed on", but I love your description.' Rishi gave me a sardonic smile.

A silence descended into our amicable chatter. Then—

'So,' said Rishi, linking his fingers behind his head, 'what's next on your Checklist?'

My insides squirmed at the very thought. I palmed the scroll from one hand to the other, pushing away the moment of unpleasantness when Satan's task would unveil itself.

'Arundathi,' Rishi said in a stern voice, 'you can't put this off.'

'Who made you my grandmother?' But I unfurled the list anyway.

My face fell. Was it possible for ghosts to grow pale, I wondered, because Rishi asked, 'What's wrong?'

I didn't think I could speak without vomiting. For a long time, I remained still and silent. Rishi's eyes filled with uncharacteristic concern for me.

'Arundathi, what is it?'

'I have to cause a "car conflagration",' I said finally in a throaty whisper.

Rishi looked aghast. '*What*? That's insane!'

'No, that's Satan.'

Drowning in the haze, I uttered five words I'd never dreamt I'd utter.

'Will you help me, Rishi?'

❦

It was noon by the time Rishi agreed to accompany me on my expedition of lunacy.

'Do you realize this could seriously throw a wrench in my plans of staying alive?' whispered Rishi.

'Don't be such a drama queen,' I drawled. 'It throws a rubber duck, max.'

We were in Shivajinagar. Shoals of urchins dotted the place. Despite it being a Sunday, the area was teeming with shoppers. What was wrong with these people, that they had dragged themselves out of bed on a weekend just to throng a place famous for its nausea-inducing powers?

I wrinkled my nose as a man spread out a dirty old blanket on the side of the road, and began arranging his wares one by one—scissors, pocket-mirrors, shaving brushes, combs, and other things that were obviously made in China.

The vendor switched on the local radio. Random news snippets blared from its outdated speakers. '*Something something* flood relief *something something* apathetic government.'

Without warning, the man spat a mouthful of paan on the road.

'That's going to put red in your aura, loser,' I muttered furiously.

'By the looks of it, I'll be joining him in Hell,' Rishi said gloomily.

'You're overthinking this.'

'I'm an abettor of a heinous crime!'

Rishi's eyes were wide and fearful. I couldn't claim much expertise in the area of placation, but I tried, anyway.

'It sounds bad if you put it *that* way. Think of yourself as…' I cast around for better words, 'a complicit participant in unpleasant pyromania.'

'Doesn't make me feel any better, Arundathi,' snapped Rishi.

'Is it because you don't know what it means?'

'Do you think condescension is going to help you?' Rishi flared up.

The vendor's radio sounded again. '*Something something* robbed bank *blah blah blah* getaway van (*rapid Kannada*) wanted list for six years.'

'Calm down, Rishi,' I said, giving the loud radio a tiny frown. 'Look, I'm not saying this is the best thing you can do to further your own reach-Heaven-or-suffer agenda, but you are *helping* me, and that's a *good* thing.'

'I'll bet that's what the Joker says to Harley Quinn every time they have something crazy in mind!'

I raised my eyebrows so high they were likely to forsake my forehead for good.

'Did you just make me your *sidekick*?'

'Sorry,' Rishi said, not sounding remotely apologetic. 'Not sidekick. Underling.'

I felt a ripple of anger. 'If I had the power, I'd have punched you!'

Rishi opened his mouth to retort, but the loud rumble of a car engine near us made his voice freeze temporarily.

'This isn't over,' he hissed, as we both turned to the newcomer in Shivajinagar.

It was a beat-up old Maruti Omni which had obviously seen better days. The car used to be white, judging by whatever was visible of its body, but age had dulled it. Patches of brown embellished its boot and front, making it look like it had been in quite a few accidents.

'Funny,' I frowned.

'Isn't it?' smirked Rishi. 'Thing belongs in *The Flintstones*. Let's set it ablaze just to put its owner out of its misery.'

I laughed distractedly, but my use of the word 'funny' hadn't been directed at the car's amusingly pathetic appearance. The smell that emanated from it... almost as if its soul was stinking of moral ambiguity.

The driver was looking down, possibly at a mobile phone. He kept mopping his forehead with a handkerchief.

'Oi.' Rishi waved his palm in front of my eyes.

'What? Did you say something?' I asked.

'I think we should make a run for it,' Rishi said urgently, sounding as if he were ready to wet his pants. His words left me deflated.

'You can't back out now!'

In the distance, the driver looked as if he might pass out.

'*Please*, Arundathi,' Rishi begged, 'think about what you're asking of me.'

'But you agreed!' I whined.

'Because I wanted you to stop Possessing my posters!'

My shoulders sagged. This wasn't going to work. Of course it wasn't. I was being stupid. How could I have assumed Rishi would assist me in something as criminal as arson?

'I'm sorry,' I said, dejected. 'I should have never dragged you into this.'

Rishi's eyes softened. 'It's okay; I can only imagine what you're going through.'

I was surprised by how gentle Rishi's voice could get.

'But I'm curious,' I frowned. 'How *do* you blow up a car?'

'How should I know?' Rishi asked. 'It's not like I spend my free time going around blowing up cars!'

I clicked my tongue. 'I'm asking you if you had any theoretical knowledge on the subject.'

'NO!'

I couldn't believe the mess I was in. I'd dragged Rishi along with me, too, hoping he'd be of some help. Despondency discovered the cracks in my confidence and slithered through them, making me wish I could die once more.

To make matters worse, despondency brought my nasty inner voice back to life.

Do not despair, my dear, it whispered. *You know whom to call.*

Go away, I pleaded. *I really don't like you.*

Nonsense, it crooned. *I am your guide. I am everywhere. Much like evil. Remember what the Middler said?*

My mind raced back. 'Evil is omnipresent', the Middler had said.

Yeah, so? I asked the voice.

So, you know whom to call to your aid now. Do it.

The voice was right, I decided after a moment. A horrible idea occurred to me.

I turned to Rishi.

'Summon a Demon,' I said, my voice flat and emotionless.

Rishi looked like I'd slapped him. 'W-what?'

'You heard me,' I said in the same voice which had never belonged to me. 'Summon a Demon. Now.'

'But... but... it's broad daylight...' Rishi struggled to find words. 'I don't t-think it's...'

Hurt him if he needs persuasion.

'You don't want me to hurt you,' I whispered. 'Do it. DO IT NOW!'

Maybe it was my voice or the prospect of finding out how a ghost could hurt a human, whatever it was, it worked on Rishi.

His shoulders shaking, Rishi closed his eyes. Leaning against a pillar in a corner, he muttered the same incantation he'd recited in the abandoned railway station.

The lines escaped his lips in a strangled croak. It sounded as if he were speaking very poor Russian. He repeated it thrice, and opened his eyes to meet mine. His shoulders weren't shaking, but he looked positively terrified.

'Maybe... maybe it didn't work,' he croaked. 'We do need a candle, and some bamboo shoo—'

'Quiet,' I ordered. Something had caught my eye.

The ground beneath us had cracked. A thin column of thick red smoke was issuing from it.

Rishi let out a terrified yelp. I watched on.

The smoke rose above us, morphing and contorting horribly as arms, legs and a torso emerged from it. A terrifying shape towered above the two of us, rearing its angry, ugly head.

'Not you again,' I groaned.

Rocky the Imp grinned, baring his teeth like a deranged wolf.

'We meet again, girly,' he growled. 'Done with the Checklist, then? Good choice! You'll go straight to Hell! I can take credit for it, an' get that raise I've been waitin' for.'

'Is this the Imp you told me about?' Rishi whimpered.

I ignored him. 'No, Rocky. I haven't made my choice. I merely summoned you here to help me out.'

'Anythin' to put you on the highway to Hell, darlin',' grinned Rocky.

'Good,' I said. My voice still had that strange hollow quality to it.

The three of us picked a spot near a public toilet. The smell was bad, but it was nothing compared to Rocky's body odour. Besides, we had to keep Rishi out of sight, and nowhere else was as deserted.

'What do you want, girly?' Rocky said. 'I don' 'ave all day.'

I took a deep breath. 'Tell me how to blow up a car.'

❦

'Cars can' just *blow up*,' Rocky snarled for the hundredth time, 'not on their ow, anyway! You would eed explosives.'

'Explain again, then!' It was important that I got everything right. There was zero room for error here.

Rocky let out an angry bellow and launched into his boring explanation which I pretended to be enraptured by yet again. 'For a car to explode there 'as to be a lot of hot fuel in a small space, an' that needs to be expelled. The best you can describe an explosive-deprived damage to a car is by saying it burned intensely. It's not a bleedin' firecracker to go boom boom.' He paused. 'It's so simple. Everyday stuff. I do it all the time.' He smirked. 'How dumb are you, don't you know *anythin'* about auto-wrecks?'

'Apart from their overdramatized usage in movies?' I rebutted.

Rocky hit his forehead in recognition of my slowness. Rishi trembled beside me. I rushed to my next question.

'So, what should happen, ideally? For a car to "burn intensely" without boom-boom?'

With great relish, Rocky sketched it out for me—petrol tanks, petrol leaks and myriad things that I had no genuine interest in. But I listened anyway, just to keep him in a good mood. It was essential that he remained calm for my next plan to set itself into motion. Every now and then, I smiled at Rishi too. Not in a warm, comforting way. In a way that suggested, 'Keep quiet, and let me do this, or watch as I feed you to Satan's moronic monster.'

'...an' that's how you make sure it goes up in smoke,' he concluded.

I let out a low whistle.

'Exactly,' nodded Rocky.

I smiled widely at the Imp. 'Thank you so much!' I rose to my feet. 'This was great, Rocky!'

Rocky got up, too, pulling Rishi by the scruff of his neck.

'Anytime, girly,' he said. 'Go do your thing. I'll keep an eye on this idiot 'ere.' He shook Rishi, dangling him a foot above the air.

Uh-oh, I thought. Summoning Rocky had been a good idea, but leaving Rishi alone with him was a little undesirable.

'Oh, that's okay, Rocky,' I said, adopting a very understanding tone. 'I'm sure you have so much to do. Tight schedule like yours and all.'

Rocky shook his head. 'No way! I wanna see you do cool stuff!'

'Are you sure? It'll be pretty boring, right? Bet you've done cool stuff like this all the time!'

But Rocky remained resolute. I cursed myself inwardly for never really having mastered the art of flattery.

I just stood there, watching Rishi taking mental steps towards passing out, and Rocky waiting for me to 'do cool stuff'. For a moment, none of us did anything. Then, everything started happening at once.

Rishi blubbered. I dived into his form, and knocked out his soul with one punch. Rocky let out a snarl of anger at my sudden disappearance.

'DUNG-BRAIN!' I yelled in Rishi's voice.

Rocky's snarl grew even louder and he took a swipe at Rishi, but I dodged the Imp's hand.

I swiftly let myself out of Rishi's body, and shouted, 'Sorry, Rishi! Just keep him distracted till I get back!'

Rishi yelled something I couldn't hear, but I was ready to bet that it was the choicest of cuss words.

Before I could be stopped by anyone, I propelled myself forward, flinging myself into the Omni driver's body.

There was a tumultuous uproar at this unholy trespass. The driver's soul immediately punched me in the face, making me see stars. Before I could regain full control again, it spit in my eye. I was enraged, and prepared to defend myself, but his soul was extremely strong. It wrestled me to the floor near the man's feet and pinned me down. Ghosts can't choke, sure, but they can feel the malicious relentlessness of another soul. I didn't want to do it, but his spirit left me with no choice. I brought my knee up to its groin and delivered the hardest blow I could, sending the soul spiralling up the man's fleshy nostrils and into a dark corner of his brain, where it remained immovably knocked out.

Rambunctious bugger, I thought.

The car was empty, and room had been cleared in the backseat for considerable luggage.

I summoned the knowledge Rocky had passed on to me in the controversial field of car torching. The driver's feverishly jittery brain showed me images of an iron rod at the base of the front seat. Relieving it from underneath, I caused enough damage to the car to render its petrol tank leaky. It didn't look remotely suspicious. To passers-by, and even Rishi, I was just an ordinary man tinkering with his near-defunct car. Nobody cared to stare curiously—after all, what help could be offered to a car that resembled a heap of metal scrap?

From the front pocket of the driver's shirt, I extracted a pack of cigarettes. I got out of the car, and, leaning against a boarded-up shop, casually lit up a cigarette. I dropped the flaming matchstick on the ground, and backed away in a flash. Making sure the man was far from the vehicle when it happened, I swiftly exited his body.

No one saw it coming.

Like a spark that sets off a firecracker, the matchstick ignited the leaking fuel. In a few seconds, giant flames shot up, their black smoke turning the clear Sunday air pungent. Debris from what was left of the Omni was flying into the air. The vehicle was ablaze, its old seats burning and becoming more useless than before.

Sudden screams turned the entire area's attention towards the flaming car. The driver's soul surfaced from its hiding place at last and, in a confused tizzy, the man took in the scenes in front of him. His eyes widened in horror at the sight of the burning car. He cursed, and fled the scene. I saw him throw his mobile phone into the burning heap as he ran.

It was time for me to get out of here, too. I flew back to

Rishi's side, and to my puzzlement, saw him standing alone. The Imp was gone.

Rishi was muttering incoherently.

'Demon ... Back ... Hell ... Father's business ... Rock E.' Word after word followed without any proper meaning.

'Hey! Rishi!' I put my fingers through his cheek.

He looked up at me, taking short breaths.

'Mission accomplished,' I said. 'Now run.'

'What?' Rishi yipped. 'Mission ... right ... huh? Why should we run?'

'Right here at Shivajinagar, in your tailored suit, you're more conspicuous than body fat on a supermodel. Believe me, you do not want to be the body fat, so, RUN!'

Everybody in the locality was screaming now. Panic reared its ugly head and roared, causing people to run helter-skelter.

'Where do we go?' Rishi asked, sounding confused.

'The safety of your house?' I suggested.

We raced to the now congested bus depot; the news of the fire had travelled like, well, wildfire.

'Jayanagar,' Rishi panted when the conductor came around.

'How many?' asked the thin man in khaki.

'Two! I mean, one,' Rishi said hastily as I shot him a warning look.

The conductor tore Rishi a ticket and walked off to the back of the bus.

Once the vehicle had filled up (which took a remarkably short time), we trundled off towards Jayanagar.

After he'd regained his breath, Rishi turned to me with a murderous expression. I gulped, even though I'd braced myself for it.

'You are so DEAD.'

On this occasion, I chose not to point out the obvious.

⚘

We got off at the bus stop and began our walk back to Rishi's house. The streets were swept bare, with withered leaves raked up against the pavement.

'Do you remember the toiletries vendor who had the radio on?' I asked Rishi.

Rishi grunted.

'Did you hear the news on the radio?'

'You did?' Rishi looked surprised.

I nodded. 'There was something about a gang of thieves who'd robbed a bank on Commercial Street. They had about fifty lakhs on them. By the sound of it, they're been planning it for months.'

'When did you hear all this?' asked Rishi in amazement.

'I have a short attention span.' I waved a dismissive hand. 'We were in conversation, and I caught words here and there. But as I was saying, these bank robbers. They'd been on the wanted list for six years. They've robbed banks in Kerala,

Andhra Pradesh and Tamil Nadu. Now, I couldn't care less about them, really, but the newsreader mentioned a getaway car. Now which route would a getaway car coming from Commercial Street take? Neighbouring Shivajinagar or the prominent main road?'

Rishi's eyes went very round.

'Are you telling me that the Omni you just wrecked was the getaway car?'

I let my lopsided grin do the answering.

'How did you know?' Rishi's voice had reached a pitch that only dogs could hear.

'The reader said it was an old van-type thing, which looked beat-up,' I responded.

'But that was an enormous risk you took!' Rishi cried. 'What if you'd got the wrong car?'

'I got it right, didn't I?' I countered dismissively.

'Arundathi,' Rishi said, skipping a broken patch on the pavement, 'you could have got someone killed.'

'How do you figure that?' I asked, tight-lipped.

'The whole thing was a gamble! You heard one snippet on the radio, heard that a getaway car was somewhere in the area, and just decided that the Omni was your target? You had a dartboard, and one dart in your hand. When the lights went out, you chucked it, and it accidentally hit the bull's eye in the dark!'

'So luck was on my side,' I shrugged. 'Happy accidents

happen all the time.'

'That is wicked,' breathed Rishi.

'No,' I corrected him with infuriating superiority. 'It's brilliant. Destroying that car might've been extremely risky, but it turned out for the best. It was gold at the end of the crossbow. *And,*' I raised my voice, because Rishi looked like he had another remark ready, 'fine, if you must know, it wasn't just a guess, alright? That driver's soul revealed that the car was the getaway car. The back seats had been cleared to allow space for the cash. So, just relax. It's fine!'

Rishi couldn't respond immediately, although I was sure he was bursting to berate me about my recklessness. I took advantage of his silence to rush to a question I was waiting to ask.

'How did you get rid of Rocky?

Rishi's brain was obviously still instructing every muscle in his face to warp in a way that fully expressed his disbelief at my highly subjective ethics. So it took him a few minutes to regain his calm and reply. 'Honestly, I don't know. The whole thing is such a blur now.' He breathed in deeply. 'I hit the panic button the second you left. That Imp kept swiping his arms, howling, and I swear, I don't think spikes are cool anymore, because two of them nearly impaled my leg.'

We were almost at Rishi's house now.

'Then, I don't know why I started talking about it, but the minute the Imp threatened to disembowel me, I started to panic big time. I started to talk utter rubbish.'

'It doesn't take an Imp from Hell to get you to talk utter rubbish,' I smirked, and then received a mutinous look from Rishi. 'Sorry, sorry, go on, I'll shut up.'

'First I started talking about climate change and how I don't think it's true, and then I went off on a tangent, and came clean about stealing test tubes and pelting first-benchers with bits of chapati when I was in school.'

'And finally, I started to talk about my father's business idea. You know, how he's planning to build all those hospitals everywhere. Somehow, it knocked the Imp out cold! Can you imagine the amount of farcical, blown up financial estimates there are in my father's plans that it had the capacity to knock out an Imp? It was insane! He yelled something about "too much competition" and disappeared into the crack in the road.'

As I shook my head in awe, Rishi opened the door to his house.

We'd barely taken two steps inside when footsteps sounded in our direction, and we were received by a man with a face as red as the wine of which he smelled.

'Where have you been?' he growled at Rishi.

Rishi's fear was palpable. 'Out,' he managed.

'Get in. Now,' said Rishi's father, his moustache quivering with rage.

Rishi said nothing. With me in tow, he stepped over the hostile threshold, the door banging shut behind him.

11

Fire and Ice

Rishi's father yelled himself hoarse about what a waste of time his son was. It went on for a long time, and included every theatrical gesture in the book. There was much shaking of fists and grinding of teeth and comparisons between Rishi and a heap of what came out of a horse's rear end.

Father and son were engaged in drama more compelling than the average soap opera.

'I send you to meet important men to help you make a future, and you go about gallivanting to nowhere? You sicken me!' Rishi's father bellowed.

'You just wanted me out of the house so you could drink yourself into a stupor!' Rishi said loudly.

'You are no son of mine!' Rishi's father spat. 'My blood does not flow in your unworthy veins!'

'Thank god for that!' roared Rishi. 'I'd die of shame if it did!'

'This is your mother's fault, the bloody woman…!'

'Don't you dare bring Ma into this!'

Rishi's father spat out half his moustache as he shouted, 'Get out of my sight!'

'Gladly!' Rishi yelled, and stormed out of the room.

I followed him in silence as he thundered up the staircase, and stomped into his room, flinging aside his mobile phone. He seemed completely unperturbed by the fact that it had come apart, its battery under the bed and the sim card lying somewhere near the study table.

'Son of a—'

'Don't,' I cautioned him. 'Messes up your aura.'

'I don't care about my aura!' Rishi snarled.

'Rishi, just calm down a little. This isn't helping you. Remember, you want to stay positive.' I switched to a language he understood. 'A red aura won't help you see God, and that's a shame because she's Scarlett Johansson's twin.'

Rishi said something like 'Pffbtt' but stopped raging.

Phew, I thought. Like father, like son.

'Do you want to talk about what happened downstairs?' I ventured timidly.

Rishi didn't say anything. He stared at his posters.

'Maybe I can help, man.' I moved a bit closer. 'Talk to me.'

Rishi looked at me with red-rimmed eyes.

'Do you know that nasty little voice in your head that's always telling you that you're not going to amount to anything?' he asked.

Past experience had taught me never to employ sarcasm in answer to a rhetorical question. I bit my tongue and let Rishi talk.

'Well, that voice is outside my head, and it's called Dad. Every damn minute of every single day. He sends me inspirational text messages, you know? Ending them with lines like "learn something from this, idiot" or "why am I sending you this, you'll junk it anyway". Does lots to improve my mood.'

Disappointment made him look pained.

'He doesn't understand that I don't want to do business! And he doesn't care either. I mean, why is it so hard to digest the fact that I don't want to be just a number in the millions? I want to earn a name for myself!'

Suddenly, I remembered what the Middler had said to me: 'You only need a name if you're going to become one'.

'You want to be seen, yeah,' I offered. 'I think I understand.'

'Glad *someone* does,' Rishi mumbled.

'Have you tried talking to him about how you feel?' I asked. 'I'm sure he cares very much about you.' I was reminded of the Middler and his father again. Maybe parents did care, they were just picky about how they did.

Rishi fixed me with a stare.

'Did you not hear him downstairs?'

'He does seem as approachable as a sabre-toothed tiger,'

I agreed, 'but you could at least try.'

Rishi sank lower into the bean bag and breathed deeply.

'He won't listen, that's for sure. Like my feelings matter. He'll ask me to shut up and do as I'm told. The last meeting he arranged for me was disastrous. I stammered throughout the business plan because my father had just shoved in into my file the night before when I was asleep, and I had no idea what it was. I was three sheets in when I realised it had something to do with hospitals.'

'So what?' I asked.

'Well,' replied Rishi morosely, 'I had started my pitch assuming the plan was for hotels.'

I offered him a grimace and he paused to pummel the bean bag.

'When I was eighteen, I told him I was entering the Arts stream. He wanted me to get into an engineering college, but my score wasn't as good as it needed to be. To pull some strings and get me into the college, he sent me to meet a paunchy man who claimed to be an honest politician…'

I let out a harsh bark of laughter. Never before had I heard the words 'honest' and 'politician' partnered outside the context of sarcasm.

'See?' Rishi piped up. 'It's funny, right? When I told my father that it was an oxymoron, he came close to slapping me. I yelled at him and stormed out of the house. I stayed at Pranav's house that night.'

'I had no idea you were going through this kind of stuff,' I said uncomfortably.

Rishi let out a hollow laugh. 'Yes well, you might have missed it somewhere between calling me Monkey Butt and Dopey Face.'

I looked at him ruefully. Rishi gave me a half-smile, and I was startled to see that he looked quite nice when he did that. I couldn't help it; I smiled too. This was a nice moment. I'd never spent time with Rishi this way. I had always been rather snappish with him. Maybe the chance to forge a strong bond with him had been lost during the time we spent bickering and fighting with each other.

It was a full minute before I realized I was staring at Rishi. Shaking myself, I looked away.

'Like what you see?' he asked slyly.

I rolled my eyes. 'Oh, please. I was lost in thought, that's all.'

'It's okay to want a piece of me,' he grinned.

'You're enjoying this, aren't you?' I said dully.

Rishi simply smiled widely. We fell silent.

'You know,' said Rishi with that same half-smile, 'I used to have a crush on you.'

My insides disappeared. 'Come again?'

Rishi nodded.

'Yeah, a long time ago. When we first met in college, I thought you were pretty, and funny too. In a way that others didn't see. I thought of asking you out on a date, but I didn't gather the courage.'

'You fancied me?' I asked incredulously. 'Rishi, no offence, but we'd have coexisted like a thorn on a rose. Or fungus on a mushroom. Or dandruff on a scalp. Or—'

'Yeah, yeah, I get it,' Rishi stopped me. 'That was very poetic, thanks.'

'Wouldn't have been *all* bad,' I told him after a pause.

Rishi shrugged.

'We'll never know, I guess.' He sighed heavily. 'Hey, here's a question: what happened to you before I summoned Rocky?'

'What do you mean?' I frowned.

'Your voice,' said Rishi. 'It went all flat and creepy and... why are you smiling like that?'

'It worked,' I said triumphantly.

'Eh? What did?'

I grinned wider still. 'There's a voice inside us, Rishi. All of us. It's what drives us to do things. Good or bad. And this voice kept telling me to seek the help of extreme evil to pull off the task of blowing up a car.' I allowed myself a grim smile. 'Except, I didn't listen to it. I only made it look like I did. So, I put on that awful voice to actually convince the inner voice that I was carrying out its evil wishes.'

Rishi looked astonished. I chortled.

'Glad to know it was convincing.'

Rishi gaped in disbelief and sunk into his bed. 'Hey, what do you think you want to do first if you ever enter Heaven?'

I thought for a brief minute and then answered. 'See my grandfather, pretty sure he's up there.'

'And?' prompted Rishi.

'And finish a game of Rummy we never got around to.' I smiled to myself. 'I abandoned our game halfway, and when I got back twelve hours later, he'd fallen asleep forever on his bed.'

'I'm sorry,' said Rishi.

'It's OK, it was a long time ago,' I said simply.

After an uncomfortable pause, I asked, 'How's Shirley? And Pranav?'

Rishi shook his head sullenly. 'You don't want to know.'

I blinked at him, not sure what to say. Knowing those two, they'd have barely got enough sleep since my death.

'You should tell Shirley you saw me,' I grinned, attempting to drag a smile back onto Rishi's face.

It worked. 'Right, so she can actually axe my head off,' he joked.

We started giggling and couldn't quite stop. I clutched my stomach as I rolled around on the floor, laughing uncontrollably. Rishi's eyes even began to water. For a while, there was only the sound of our own cackling.

Rishi finally wiped his eyes and looked at me. Suddenly, his eyebrows shot up in alarm, and he stopped laughing.

'What's happening to you?'

'What do you mean?' I looked down at my hands, still chortling. They were fluctuating between red and gold. I looked like a bunch of malfunctioning fairy lights.

With a pang that wiped the mirth off my face, I remembered that I'd exhausted the number of tasks on the Checklist. My hand immediately flew to my back pocket. The Checklist was gone!

'Your aura is flickering,' Rishi observed. 'What's going on?'

'My time is up,' I declared calmly.

I didn't know why I felt so matter-of-fact about it. Was I subconsciously waiting for this moment? Three days had gone by in a flash. My brief stint as a ghost on earth were over.

'You're leaving? Now?' Rishi asked me unhappily. 'Do you absolutely have to?' he added.

'I suppose I do,' I said, just as I felt a tug near my navel.

'Will you come visiting?' Rishi asked.

'Sure, if I'm granted access to Earth ever again!' I replied, as if we were having a normal conversation about visiting Disneyland.

Without warning, I began to ascend and make my way towards the mullioned windows. Rishi hurriedly opened them, but it wouldn't have mattered anyway, for I soared right through.

My thoughts were as cloudy as the sky above. I both wanted and didn't want to leave. But the ascension didn't stop.

'If you come back, I'll call Shirley and Pranav, we'll make it a party,' he said as I hovered high above his house.

'Yeah, it'll be fun,' I called back. 'What a boo-tiful reunion it will be!'

'Arundathi!' Rishi's tone was urgent.

I looked down and met his eyes.

'How come you wore that necklace for me?' he asked, his voice cracking a little.

I smiled wistfully. 'Because I knew you'd be the only one who'd really believe it was me, the only one who'd really see me. And I just wanted to be seen.'

❦

As a child, I'd always wanted to fly out of windows and soar into the sky like Peter Pan. It was slightly unfortunate to have had that dream fulfilled after death.

The return journey to the Middle Land seemed to be far shorter than reaching Earth. I remembered what the Middler had said about the incoming traffic of ghosts that caused a hold-up in the skies every day, and I hoped with all my might to never encounter it.

Thankfully, the clouds were clear of traffic. Or maybe those souls had been redirected by the traffic cop, Imp Kotumai.

Within a minute, it seemed, I reached the Middler's residence with a 'poof'!

'Well, well, well,' came his voice from behind a misty curtain. He stepped out of it dramatically, twirling a baton. 'If it isn't Little Miss Snarky.'

'You look like a court jester,' I pointed out.

'And you,' he regarded my aura with a critical eye, and then grinned wickedly, 'ah, *you*...'

He didn't finish that sentence, for at that very moment, a gong sounded. I couldn't determine exactly from where it had come. It sounded as if it had blasted from all around, like those awful loudspeakers during Ganesh Chaturthi.

There was a grating crackle of static, and then, a familiar male voice spoke.

'Hurry up, we had you scheduled for lunch.'

I looked at the Middler, chewing my lip in apprehension.

'Is that who I think it is?' I squeaked.

'No, it's not Hannibal Lecter.'

I ignored his comment. Swallowing hard, I made my solitary way to the Choosing Commons. The gates were thrown open already, and beyond the garden entrance stood God and Satan.

She was wearing an unembroidered gown of green silk today while Satan had thrown on a pair of breezy shorts and a casual tee. It was hard to look at him and not drool.

Get a grip, dumbo, I chided myself. It's his hypnotic power!

I chose to gaze at the trees instead.

'So, Arundathi,' God said, her gown billowing slightly in the wind, 'here you are again.'

I nodded, wishing I had something cleverer to say.

'And by the looks of it, we're back to square one,' said Satan, his voice as cold as steel.

'Say what?' I frowned.

'Your aura's cleanly divided between red and gold again,' spat Satan. 'What a monumental waste of my time. I'm burning you.'

He started towards me, but God held him back with a whippy wave of her hand.

'No,' she said sharply. 'Arundathi, I sense you *have* made a choice...'

I didn't refute her.

My mind wandered through the confusing labyrinth that had been the last three days of my afterlife. The incidents of good and evil I'd been part of popped up in my mind's eye like advertisements in a YouTube page.

Every memory of my dark inner voice nudging me in the direction of evil made me want to recoil in horror. I couldn't believe it was a part of me. I remembered that one horrid encounter with Satan's minion, Rocky, which had resulted in a blood-red aura. I'd never forget the intense loathing I'd felt for myself after I'd given in to the seductive power of rage, an ever-present temptress. I thought of Shalini, and my shame deepened. These memories flooded my thoughts and I felt utterly sickened, wanting nothing more than to curl up and fall into an endless sleep.

But then I thought of the girl on the scooter, how her eyes had shone with gratitude. I remembered the cake, the homeless man and even Saran. I longed to relive those moments—they filled me with warmth. I reflected on how difficult a task it was to explain even to myself how nice I'd felt after doing good. The sheer inadequacy of words in capturing the feeling of an almost divine goodness that had accompanied carrying out God's task to the word…

I did know what to say to God, after all. I looked into her beautiful, expectant eyes, and stated it firmly.

'I'll take that halo if you have it.'

God smiled. Satan let out a cry of fury.

'NO! Bloody girl! I waited twenty stinking years to claim you! It was foretold you had great potential to spread evil in the nine realms of our world! CURSE THE FATES! I'll have your kneecaps for this!'

A lethal-looking black trident glittered to form between his fingers, and he chucked it at me.

I had no time to respond. But I didn't have to, for God shot forward to my rescue, and swatted the trident aside without much effort.

'Lay one finger on Arundathi, and you will wish you hadn't dragged yourself out of the Underworld,' God whispered, in a calm, controlled manner.

'I work out, woman. I can knock you out!' challenged Satan.

'Bring it, Horn-Head,' snarled God. 'I do yoga.'

Suddenly, the ground shook, unable to take the energy the two powers were summoning.

God's gown melted away to reveal a battle suit, complete with armour—a shield was latched to her back, and she clasped a spear in her hand. Behind her, snow-capped mountains appeared with howling tornados nesting at their peaks. The giant powder blue eagles perched themselves on top of trees not too far from her, ready to take flight at the word go. At the foot of the mountains, pools of water splashed, with armed mermaids breaking the water surface, rearing to go. Angels descended by the hundreds, each of them looking unexpectedly menacing. (One of them looked slightly punch drunk, and was struggling with her grip on her sitar.) And to my utter surprise and delight, Saran and V appeared at God's side.

Meanwhile, Satan morphed into a red beast with smooth scales covering his torso. Tiny horns stuck up sharply on his head and a spiky tail slithering from his back. He was backed by an army of slithered snakes, jet black and venomous. Large Imps formed ranks behind him, readying cannons and wielding lethal maces. Rocks dropped into Satan's landscape; sharp-edged, unfriendly boulders of death, surrounded by pools of steaming lava.

Both sides stood perfectly still. And then, in the tense silence, a cannonball soared into the air with an ominous sound, and flew past an eagle, missing it by a fraction.

The eagle screeched, and all hell broke loose.

The two armies charged at each other as the Commons turned into a battlefield. I ran for shelter. A tree near one of God's mountains grew before my very eyes and sent down its branches, creating a protective sanctuary around me and giving me an excellent view of the battle too.

The eagles were merciless. They flew down on the serpents, pecking at them without any mercy. In a flash of blue and black, the adders slithered on the ground, hissing madly as their eyes were gouged out by the mighty birds. The Imps were ruthless. They dived into the pools near the mountains and braved the holy waters to fight the mermaids. Spike after spike went through the fish-tailed creatures, but they defended themselves until the last of the Imps were injured and had retreated.

V was spectacular. She somersaulted all over the place, snatching green demons off the ground with each cartwheel. By the time she was done with her routine, she had demons bound and gagged with unbreakable rainbows. Some of these demons seemed to have been petrified, and I suspected that V's perfume had powers beyond imagination.

Saran, too, was in his element. He was racing through the armies of Satan, shooting arrows at everything that dared to confront him. When a particularly roguish demon attacked him, tearing his leather jacket, he was furious. 'MY LEVIS'!' he bellowed, and released a bright red arrow with his bow.

It flew past me and lodged itself in the demon's armpit. At once, the demon collapsed, but far from writhing in pain, it rolled on its side, a simpering look overcoming its face. The creature threw caution to the wind, and started spouting romantic verse.

'What the hell was that?' I asked Saran, my voice loud above the din around us.

'I raided father's quiver!' Saran shouted back, already nocking an arrow and taking careful aim at an approaching demon. 'Cupid's Cluster—very powerful series. Renders one senseless!'

He didn't see me giving him a thumbs-up as he sprinted off to take down the rest of the army.

There seemed to be no end to the battle. But no sooner had I thought that thought, than the dust settled, and the noise dulled down. Through the thinning clouds of destruction, I could see the result of the battle: Satan's forces were completely beaten.

Satan let out a deafening roar, and his wrath broke out on them. They fizzled out in puffs of green smoke, filling the air with an acrid, burning smell.

Without preamble, Satan charged at God, his poisonous claws out and his fangs bared.

He lunged at God, but she stepped aside in the last minute, causing him to skid to a sudden stop and spin around midway. Like a leopard, he raged and lunged again. This time, even though God was quick to avoid his pounce, he managed to rip through the armor. She eyed Satan with a calculating look, to anticipate his next move. Satan was sweating and panting, lunging this way and that, while all God did was escape his attacks. She didn't appear to be the least bit worn out.

Satan took on the form of a man with four hands, far more bestial that the animalistic appearance he had adopted earlier. He held up his hands and conjured frightening balls of black fire. With a mighty cry, he tossed them at God. She summoned a tornado from the mountains and flung the fire out of her way. They landed on a tree and caused it to burst into a million sparks of eerily orange light. Letting out a murderous cry, God advanced. I noticed that the tips of her fingers were glowing silver.

'Stop playing around and fight me!' snarled Satan. 'Fight me like a man!'

'I'll do you one better.' God's eyes were slits of malice and disgust. 'I'll fight you like a woman.'

God waved her fingers at the ground and produced a snowflake. The prettiest blue-white snowflake I'd ever seen.

'A snowflake?' sneered Satan. 'That's what you call to your aid? A pretty little snowflake?'

God's lips curved into a dangerously beautiful smile.

'Snowflakes are pretty,' she raised her arm, 'until they come together to form an avalanche.'

The mountains behind her rumbled with a deafening sound. Their snow-capped tops ascended into the sky, and with a swing of God's commanding arm, came rushing forth.

A howling sound, a flying wall of snow and a yell of shock later, Satan was trapped under a white bed of the prettiest blue-white precipitation I'd ever seen. I couldn't stop myself; I let out a 'whoop!' of ecstasy.

God snapped her fingers, and the jagged rocks that had appeared on Satan's order, manifested next to him. Before Satan could escape God pinned him against them and forced him into golden shackles. In a flash, she had Satan bound and gagged, and fettered to the rocks.

Satan grunted loudly, unable to speak. His eyes were mirrors of foul images of tortured souls burning in his chamber.

'Your special effects do not intimidate me,' said God, adjusting the straps over her shoulders. Her armour had vanished, and she was back in her gown.

'Nor me,' I added, stepping beside God. Her warmth made me feel as light as air.

I bent low to look at Satan.

'You are treacherous. Reeking of darkness, it is no wonder you seek to destroy others. You sent that Imp to sway events in your favour. That's cheating. And cheaters never prosper.'

I straightened up and felt God's proud arm around my shoulders.

'Your abode is nothing but a dungeon of despair,' I said to the Devil. 'I have no trouble believing that I'd suffer there. So, thanks, but no thanks—I have no interest in joining you in Hell. I'm only interested in playing on a winning team.'

Satan glared at me, his ears beginning to expel heat waves.

'Oh dear,' sighed God. 'He's planning to blow up the place.' She looked at me with a twinkle in her eyes. 'I rather think we've spent enough time here, don't you?'

'Yes, I do,' I said smiling.

Together, we turned our back on Satan and walked off towards the pearly gates which shimmered beyond a beautiful apple orchard.

At the gates, something struck me.

'God, I'll be right back.'

'Where are you going?' she enquired.

But I didn't answer. I retraced my footsteps to the Commons. Satan was still trapped, trying to spit out the rag stuffed in his mouth. He made a growling noise when he caught sight of me.

I picked up the fallen trident. It felt abnormally heavy in my hands. Probably the weight of those souls it had tormented over centuries.

I positioned myself at a reasonable distance from Satan, and took careful aim. I raised the trident as threateningly as a marksman would knock an arrow.

With a glint in my eye, I released the weapon. It sliced the air cleanly and hit Satan between his eyes.

Doing an about turn, I drifted away with a backward glance. If I'd looked at the rocks, I would've seen a fizzing cloud of red vapour, and a burning tail.

God stood at the pearly gates, her smooth forehead creased with thin lines.

'What did you go back for?' she asked.

I smiled with a bright twinkle in my eyes.

'To do good, of course.' I grinned and followed her past the gates, into somewhere I finally belonged.

Epilogue

'This beard is getting out of control,' he said.

'Yes, you're a regular Santa Claus,' I said, not even glancing at him. 'Now, make your move.'

'Patience, child,' the old man said slowly. 'Time, to you, is an endless resource now.'

I grunted. He was always full of gems like these. I popped some white cotton candy into my mouth; the place was famous for it.

After several minutes, the old man pulled a card from his set and threw it down between us.

I grunted again.

'What use do I have for this?' I muttered and drew a card from the stacked set.

I played a lousy hand and glanced at my grandfather, who was smiling.

'I believe a seven of Spades completes my sequence, thank you very much.' He placed his cards down to reveal a winning set.

'I win. *Again*,' he declared.

'Best of forty-two?' I suggested meekly.

He laughed airily. It was such a nice sound.

'Alright, then,' he agreed, as he picked up the deck to shuffle the cards.

As his hands worked, I looked outside at the patchwork of snow-capped mountains, tall oaks and meandering streams. Deep green woods adorned the landscape, with cabins like gingerbread houses nestled in secret corners. Little bridges curved over stony brooks as fireflies danced in twilight. A sheet of tulips swayed in the wind down in a cosy valley.

'What do you see outside, Grandpa?' I asked him out of curiosity.

He turned his attention to the world outside.

'You. Pigtailed, in a frock, running free in a banana plantation outside our ancestral home. I see my old rocking chair, set against the backdrop of a tea estate, where the lush green stretches across the lands. Savithri is there, too, bringing me a tumbler of coffee.'

I smiled at him. 'Is that your Heaven?'

My grandfather pondered the question, and said, 'I suppose. Heaven is, after all, whatever you want it to be.'

I gazed upon his wizened old face for a few minutes before thumbing through my deck and setting myself a sequence for our game of Rummy.

There was a gentle knock on the door, and a young girl

dressed all in white stepped into our room.

'Arundathi?'

I looked up. 'Yeah?'

'You have work to do,' she said, handing me a tiny scroll.

I unfurled the parchment and checked my to-do for the day. It seemed like fairly routine work.

'I'll get right on it,' I told the girl.

Crossing into my room, I changed into soft white linens, and adjusted the halo over my head.

'Grandpa,' I called from the front door, 'I'll be right back. The World needs saving.'

I hovered out into the open sky, where the Middler stood talking to a sobbing ghost of a woman. Her aura was half-red, half-gold.

'Hey, Maddy,' I called.

The Middler turned to me, smiling slightly. It'd been weeks since I'd started calling him by his real name, and he still wasn't used to it.

'What?' he asked, in his usual drawl.

'I forgot to return this to you.' I fished the necklace out of my pocket. 'Here.'

Maddy shook his head. 'I think people see me just fine, then?'

'Enjoy your dinner with your father tonight!' I smiled.

With that, I soared out of my cloudy home with my wings spread out wide, all set to add a tinge of gold in someone's aura.

Printed in the USA
CPSIA information can be obtained
at www.ICGtesting.com
CBHW021154150824
13133CB00011B/225